COLT

An MC Romance (Outlaw Souls Book 6)

HOPE STONE

GET FREE BOOKS!

Join Hope's newsletter to stay updated with new releases, get access to exclusive bonus content and much more!

Join Hope's newsletter here.

Tap here to see all of Hope's books.

Join Hope's Readers Group on Facebook.

PROLOGUE

Four and a Half Years Ago

"You have the parts?"

"Yeah, I do. When can I pick them up?"

"You got 'till noon tomorrow. They'll be available at the usual meeting spot. Bring the truck around back, and make sure you're alone. You have half an hour to load up."

I responded with a slow head nod. I understood the steps. I'd been following them for months without a hiccup. "Done. See you then."

The Merced sun was showing no mercy, beating down on the back of my neck. At the ripe old age of thirty-five, my bones ached as if they were attached to a fifty-year-old. I should have been used to the burning heat. After all, I grew up as a California farm boy, and I still lived on the farm.

I would sit by the brook some days as a teenager and watch the rocks skim over the water. That was when I wasn't getting on and falling off of horses.

A man I'd looked up to all my life—Clive Winters, my father—would tell me every time I fell off, "You are not going to let that horse get the best of you, now are you? I didn't raise a softie. Come now, son. Get back on the horse."

PROLOGUE

I smiled wryly. I used to think he was surely out to get me, to see me fail. Now I knew something entirely different.

I wouldn't give up my country lifestyle for anyone. I remembered how the red, tawny dirt swirled in the air while I straddled the paddock fences, rebuilding them from years of wear and tear. All that work on the farm gave me the strength of a lion. That strength was distributed on my six-foot-one frame nicely. My hair was pretty shaggy and bleached blond from the Cali sun. I remembered the distant calls of wild coyotes in the cool of the night.

On my farm, we ran with ten chickens, and all of them laid. One old rooster, affectionately known as Croak, was the alarm for first light and dusk. The horses on the farm were my pride and joy. I spent the most time with them. I had three purebred caramel Palominos and one sleek black mare.

We grew all sorts of products on the farm, too—carrots, onions, strawberries, and green beans. I'd taken over the farm from my tired and weary parents in my late twenties. My parents were in their sixties, and they both wanted a break.

"We want you to run the farm, son. Carry on the Winters name. Think you can do that for us?" my father asked me one day.

"Yep. I got you, Pop," I'd said. "I wouldn't have it any other way."

I knew the farm and the lay of the land like the back of my hand, and I had since I was a kid. That became that. We got the papers signed so that the farm was in my name, and I kept successfully running it. I managed to run the place with a firm but fair hand and a tight-knit crew who were loyal to the Winters. When the end of the crop season finished, they all received nice bonuses to take home to their families.

My other love, motorcycles, gave me the same freedom my horses did, which is why I had a custom chopper with a stallion drawn on the chrome. The moonlight sat behind the

PROLOGUE

horse, which was rearing, its front legs in the air. When my bike developed some problems, I took her into the Merced motorcycle repair shop. That's how I first linked up with the Outlaw crew. They were a really cool crew. So I joined and didn't think too much about it. I got my vest a while later, thinking it was just a crew I would ride with every now and then. As time wore on, the business was revealed to me.

"Hey, we got a job for you if you're interested." Vlad, the Outlaw Souls enforcer, stood solid, tall, and deadly in the warehouse quarters I worked at. It was a chop shop with really good prices for customers. Again, I didn't think anything of it, and I didn't ask any questions. I probably should have.

"Sweet. What's the job?" The farm was kind of slow at that time of year since we were between crop seasons.

"I need you to collect some auto parts and ship them down to La Playa. Ortega Autos are going to utilize them." When Vlad spoke, you listened. He represented death. His eyes penetrated your soul, and his dark aura let you know what time it was. He wasn't the guy you wanted to fuck with.

"Say no more. Where are the pickups running from?"

"They're running out of an old warehouse in Merced. I'll give you the address. All you have to do is the stock inventory and organize the shipments. I've already set up the deal with my Russian counterparts."

"Okay. Sounds like a sure bet."

He pressed his large hand on my shoulder.

"It is a sure bet. Just don't fuck it up. These guys are executioners by trade, and they don't give two fucks about shooting you in the head. You'll get a monthly kickback. Should help you with the farm expenses." Vlad winked.

"Sure would be nice. I could use the help right now. Things are a little tight between seasons. Plus, I have Bella's

PROLOGUE

kindergarten fees coming up. Anna is working a little, but not much."

Vlad winked again and readjusted his leather jacket. "Thought as much, which is why I offered you the job."

Anna was my Bella's mother and a real fiery brunette rebel from the streets. Despite her flaws and for all her bravado, I could always see through to the heart of her, and that thing was golden, just like the California hills. I'd taken her off the streets. She was a meth cook, and since Bella had been born, she seemed to have settled into her purpose in life. On that day, like any other in Merced, I kissed her goodbye in the morning.

"Bye, baby. Have a great day," she said, and I bent my head to her lips. "Bella, say bye to Daddy. He has to go to work now."

The innocence of my baby girl softened every part of my heart as I held her in my arms. Her sandy brown hair was in pigtails. Her big brown eyes were the same color as her mother's, but she had my tight cheekbones. Her tiny lips reached the side of my cheek for a peck.

"Okay. Daddy has to go earn the bacon. See you and Mommy tonight." I grinned at her.

"Okay, Daddy. I love you. You can put me down now."

She wriggled free of my arms, and I laughed. There was never a dull day with four-year-old Bella.

The dirt scuffed my tan leather cowboy boots as I kissed my horses goodbye in the stables, a morning ritual I'd carried with me since my days on the farm with my father.

Today was the standard pick-up day. Nothing shaking. A normal day like any other. I straddled and mounted my bike, heading into the Merced warehouse. When I pulled up, the radio was blaring, and the warehouse door was open.

Diego greeted me with a smile. "Hey, brother. How you doing?"

PROLOGUE

"Doing great. About to head out to this pick-up. We are moving these parts hard. Must be a lot of repairs coming out of La Playa."

Diego, with his dirty blond hair, blew out a breath. Diego was the maestro of bikes. He could bring any bike back to life. He'd built the chapter from the ground up, and now it was forty members deep. He stood another inch taller than me, and if you didn't know us well, you would say we were brothers. Diego's Argentinian heritage made him a shade darker than me, though.

"You're telling me. There is a ludicrous amount of parts being used. They need more people in the chop shop. It's so busy. They ain't got the room. I run my motorcycle repair shop, though, so I don't want to be involved with the parts."

"For real? Guess it's cheap for La Playa. We are getting them at a heavily discounted rate. As far as being involved goes, sometimes you just have to do what you have to do." I sneered.

"You got that right."

"Okay, I'm going to go ahead and ride out. The truck here yet?"

Diego wiped down one of the bikes he was working on, stepping back to assess it.

"Yup. It's out back. Here are the keys. Be careful. The only reason I'm giving them to you is that Vlad isn't here." He reached in his pocket and threw the keys at me.

With one hand, I caught them.

"See you when you get back."

I strolled to the small truck and cranked the engine. On the way over, my stomach turned. A pressure sat in the cavern of my lungs as the green and gold California hills rolled by. As I approached the gate, my breathing became labored. I pulled into the warehouse and reversed in for easy access. I had the key to the roller door, but for some reason, it was already

PROLOGUE

open. That sinking feeling came back. Maybe they'd left it open, ready for me. I sat in the truck for a minute, shaking off the paranoia.

Languidly, I let my cowboy boots hang out the side and stepped out of the truck. I came around the back and opened the latches. The warehouse was cold and dark. Again, nothing to worry about. A standard at this stage. Only two Russians met me, and they stood in the dark with long leather jackets and gloves on. Only the long strip of light from the outside door made them visible.

"Good. You're on time," I quipped.

"We got those parts you need."

"Perfect, I'll get them right now." I started toward the back of the truck. In the shadows, I witnessed their horror-stricken faces along with mass confusion.

"What's the problem?" I asked them.

I missed the light footsteps behind me, but I didn't miss the barrel of the pistol to the side of my temple. I balled my hands into fists, ready to knock this motherfucker out.

Then the words of the law rang through my ears. "Freeze! You're under arrest. Put your hands in the fucking air, now!"

Several navy blues raided the place like worker ants, snatching the duffel bag from my fingers. The two Russians looked at me closely. One of them mouthed, "Don't snitch," and ran a line across the bottom of his chin.

I put my hands behind my head, and all I saw was Bella and her cute toothy smile flashing through my brain. Anna and her raven hair. I didn't know if she would cope if I went in. I couldn't hear their muffled voices as they read me my rights. They faded away at that point. The sirens and the lights surrounded me as I said nothing. On that day, my luck ran out, and so did my time.

COLT

"Let's go, cell block six! You got half an hour in the yard! Let's go. Let's go!" a burly prison guard's voice perforated D-block.

The warning came just before the cell doors clicked open. I licked my chapped lips and stepped out of my cell cautiously. I bent my head down and stepped straight into line. That was the drill. I did a headcount and saw that about thirty other guys were being let out to the yard or the common area. One small window of freedom is all we got every day at USP Atwater. I welcomed the time out. My spot in the jail was cemented, so nobody would touch me. When I first came in four and a half years ago, I'd had to prove my spot really quickly.

The sneers had come through the cell bars when I'd arrived.

"Look at this, Roger. We got ourselves a new little bitch to play with."

A jail roughneck who was known for making new inmates his playtoys got the word of my arrival. I looked that motherfucker in the eyes as I passed his cell.

"Listen up, you piece of shit. I'll kill your mother, your father, your brothers, your cousin, and anyone else that tries it in here. You hear

me?" I let him feel the cold chill of my eyes on his face while I held the fury of twenty men in my balled-up fists. He took a beat to size me up.

"Tough guy, huh? You talk like that, you must know something," he replied, lifting his chin at me.

He was a huge guy with shoulders like small boulders merged into his neck. He gave me a gruesome smile with his big dirty eyes. From the looks, he wasn't in the pen for armed robbery. He had a quote tattooed across his neck and multiple face tattoos. I knew his type. Plus, he was too big to take me down. Prison law versus street law was different, I found out.

"You got that right. I'm an Outlaw 'till the day I die," I yelled loudly as I passed the guy's cell.

The weedy guard who brought me in was silent the whole time. He opened my rusty cell door, where one other guy lay on a bolted bunk bed. In the corner was a single basin. The tap dripped continuously, and the toilet smelled, well, like shit. One single TV on a swivel was up high in the corner. The faint lime green paint was peeling off the walls, and a few books were stacked on two simple shelves.

"Welcome to your new home for the next five years," the prison guard snarked as he pushed me in the back and into the hellhole.

So any time I could get out of the cell was my version of heaven.

I moved around a small grassed area with four walls. It was big enough to fit about fifty men comfortably. The first thing I did was stretch out my neck and look up at the open blue sky. Not far from me was a weight bench that had two guys getting in their reps. I knew them. I'd seen them in the yard a time or two. Both of them were in for petty-theft type charges, nothing life-altering.

"C'mon, Marty. We got three to go. Max rep sets."

Grunts came from the guy underneath the barbell as he strained to lift. I watched as the veins pulsed against the side of his neck, threatening to burst. Eventually, he heaved the barbell off his chest.

One other guy toward the back of the jail was skipping in a nice rhythm, dripping sweat on the grimy pavement. A stiff-looking correctional officer stood in the corner, watching us all like a hawk. He had a baton firmly slotted in his holster and a taser on the other side. His mouth was opening and closing with the gum he was popping.

The guard's name was Chester, and he was a complete sucker. If I got my farm hands on him on the outside, I would have snapped his neck in half like we snapped our chickens' necks back in the day. Chester put me in the hole for three days for this one time when I got in a scrap. That shit wasn't my fault. The guy tried to pull a fucking razor out on me. That's before I knew the prison hierarchy game. I flashed back to the memory, not a time I would forget easily.

"You talking back, boy?" Chester had hissed in my ear.

He had me in a strong chokehold. My air supply was tied up as I grabbed his forearm to release it for breath. Lopez, being the bitch he was, tried to blame me for his drug shipment being smuggled into the wrong cell. Yes, you could still run drugs in the jail, provided you were in good with the correctional officers.

I was well-matched, physically, to take Lopez. He was about six foot tall like me, heavily muscled, and quick with his speech and movements. He ran with a drug crew on the streets called the Merced Mercenaries. A lone teardrop sat right under his left eye. His caramel complexion and honey-colored eyes made him a target for those who wished he would drop the soap in the showers. He didn't worry about that, as he was the drug insider and supplied over half the jail, including the correctional officers.

"Heard you knew about the shipment, and you moved it, player." The right side of Lopez's mouth turned up as he spoke to me before Chester came in.

He'd just walked into the door with his hands balled into fists. The washing machines whirred around us as I finished folding my laundry. No other people were in the laundry room at that time. In jail, that was usually a no-no. Witnesses were needed for everything. Otherwise, it didn't happen. I calmly picked up one of the white sheets from the dirty laundry basket and wrapped it around my hand.

My back tensed up as Lopez circled. I let my peripheral vision govern his footwork.

"Oh yeah? Where you hear that? Because I don't have anything to do with your little operation," *I replied slowly.*

"I know you're not about to do nothing with that sheet. I fucking know you're not."

Lopez closed the laundry door behind him. I heard the lock click as he moved a step toward me. I bent my knees and hunched in position. I scanned his body for weapons. He spat out a razor from the side of his mouth. It shot right into his hand. He held up the gleaming piece of metal and grinned.

"See this? This here is what I got for boys like you."

He looked away briefly but lunged at the same time, trying to catch me unaware. I retracted my head back as the breeze from his swing tried to connect with my face. I let out a whooshing sound. I circled with him, and we started to dance.

"Snow told me you slashed his face. So you think you're gonna do that to me?" *I teased. My hands hung low on both sides, and I stretched my fingers out, ready to pop him in the jaw. I looked at his body. It was wide open.*

"That's right, bitch. Now it's your turn."

Lopez lunged. I saw the metal pass the right side of my face. I bumped into the side of the washing machine, and the edge jabbed me in the side. I held it for a quick minute.

Lopez grinned as his eyes narrowed. He swiped again, and this time, I tunneled my left fist into his lower intestine. He coughed as the impact made him draw up into himself and set him back a few feet.

"How do you like that? Huh? I fucking told you I ain't got nothing to do with your drugs."

He yelped, "You bastard."

He staggered, and I thought that would be the last of it. He put his foot out near my left leg, and my foot came out from under me. I fell on one knee to the ground. I tried to stabilize with one hand, but I wasn't quick enough. He ran the razor across the edge of my neck. My reflexes made it so that it was just a nick, but I felt the blood trickle down my throat. The red shadow of rage pounded behind my eyes, sending me into overdrive. I burrowed my head into his stomach, blasting him into the back of the washing machine on the other side of the room.

I felt the air run out of his lungs as he slumped to the ground, and the razor fell to the concrete slab. The siren went off, and my eyes flew to the camera in the corner. I quickly approached the door to leave, but on the other side was Chester. He put his hand out.

"Stop right there! What the fuck is going on?" He took one look at Lopez slumped in the corner and one at me.

"I was defending myself! I swear."

He came straight for me and laced me in a chokehold. "You're going to simmer down in solitary confinement, Outlaw. This is my prison, and we don't let shit like that fly."

That was my first-year introduction. I would never forget it.

Now, one stationary camera in the back left hand side focused on the yard's activity. Not all thirty men came to the yard. Some others went to the common area, a dilapidated room the size of two living rooms and not enough space for a thousand inmates to congregate. That's too much testosterone for one area. I wanted to get some sets in and talk to some of the old-timers in the yard.

I strolled over to Austin, who was holding the barbell for another guy. Austin was a tough Mexican in his sixties but strong as an ox. His eyes and ears were to the ground in the prison, and he knew everything. I placed the barbell back in its slot as the guy lifted his head off the bench.

Austin, with his scrappy gray beard and bald head, smiled a lopsided grin as I came toward him.

"Hey, young buck. How are you holding up?" He raised his bushy brow at me as he adjusted his gloves.

I pointed at him. "Stay right there. I want to talk to you about something. I need a spot, too."

Austin nodded and waited until I got under the bar. "You want to know how you can get a message to Frank, right?" He leaned over the bar and turned back to the guard.

"Damn straight," I said as I flattened my back against the bench with my feet firmly on the ground.

"Okay. What's the message, young buck?" Austin knew my weights and slid the heavy steel plates on either end of the bar.

"No message. I need face to face. That's my Outlaw brother. I know he's coming out of the hole from last month. That place will send you to your grave early."

Austin's grave laugh rang out. "You got that right. Solitary is the place for no one. If your mind doesn't get you, the rats will. Can't see your food, either, when they slide it through the hole. They probably spit in it. Many have hung themselves down there. You learned to stay away from Lopez, though others might not have. His sole mission was to send inmates to solitary, and if he viewed you as a threat, he started trouble deliberately. The guards were in on it, too. That's why Chester knew when to come in like he did. You're not special. It's their one-two combination. I'm glad that sorry son of a bitch got transferred."

"Me too. He was out to get me from the jump. He knew I was an Outlaw."

"Uh-huh," Austin responded in recognition.

I shook my head as I felt the weight bear down on me. My arms shook with the new test of the extra weight that Austin had added this time.

"That's it. Hold it. You got it. Lower down slow. Let's go. I'm testing you today."

I sucked in and exhaled on the push up. At three-quarters of the way up, Austin took the weight. He threw me the towel to wipe my face.

"So you ain't a snitch, huh?" he asked.

"Nope. That's not how we do it in the Outlaws. Got me five years, but I just have to keep my nose clean for the next six months, you know?"

"Could have been no years. Vlad made a situation for you. Frank told me."

"I know, but now he owes me. No better situation than to be in the driver's seat."

"That depends on you making it out of here alive. Now, let me tell you something. These jerks can smell when you're about to get close to being let out. They're going to try and rock you, to make it hard. They'll try to corner you and get more stacked on your sentence. I wouldn't be coming out to the yard anymore if I were you. Just lay low."

Austin lifted the weight down on my chest again as I set up for the second set. He lowered as my arms burned from the lactate build-up. I inhaled on the drop and exhaled, straining hard on the lift. Austin put his fingertips under and didn't lift the burden. I thought the weight would drop on my chest.

"C'mon now. Quit being a pussy. You got it in you. C'mon."

I grunted with the last drop of force I had, lifting the bar an inch higher. Austin assisted from there.

"There you go. We'll make one out of you yet."

The adrenaline from lifting kept me sane in this hell hole, and it felt good to have some of that now. "I hear you about staying low. I just have this one thing I have to get done before I leave here, and I know Frank can help me."

"No doubt he can. I'll set it up and send word to you."

Austin watched the guard as he made the rounds around the perimeter of the yard.

"I don't know how you've made it all these years in here, Austin."

Austin laughed. "I've weathered bitter storms, my boy, but none greater than losing my wife in the summer of eighty-nine. I didn't care to live after that, anyway."

"You shot the perp nine times. That's crazy," I replied. I knew of Austin's story through my cellmate. It was one for the books.

Austin whistled through his teeth. "Yup, that's what happens when shit goes sideways. That guy tried to come for my baby. I had to avenge her. I didn't know the guy would keep a gun in the house."

Austin had received life in prison for the murder. He knew most of the lifers in the pen.

"Put me in touch with Frank. I want to talk to him."

Austin, with his humble and wise eyes on mine, nodded. "Okay. Consider it done, Colt."

AMBER

I packed up my yellow manila case file folders, gathering them from my desk. All of my questionnaires and profiling information were prepared for the visit. My job as a social worker was a time-consuming part of my life, but I loved it. I stood for justice, especially if it involved kids. This particular case involved a little cutie who was turning seven in a couple of months.

"My daddy's in prison. I think he did something bad," she'd said to me on my first visit to see her. I remembered her sitting with her finger in her mouth on her grandmother's lap. She pleaded with her warm brown eyes. "I want him to come home. Will you bring my daddy home?"

Bella, the poor little girl, had a lot to contend with.

My thick blond hair was down and just below my shoulders. The Merced heat made it unbearable to be touching the back of my neck, so I opened my top drawer and placed it in a ponytail. Our office sat in the middle of downtown Merced. It was a small office with individual cubicles. On my desk, I had a few quotes pinned up to remind me why I did the job in the first place. I fingered the leaves of my potted plant, which

I'd affectionately named Josie. Her leaves were looking a little dusty and dry.

"Sorry, Josie. I've neglected you again. Mama's got a little water for you. My bad," I whispered softly to my plant as I grabbed the bottled water I had left on my desk. I read somewhere that if you talked to your plants, it would help them grow faster, and they would be healthier. I poured the water into Josie's rich earthy soil and smiled.

Lucy came by at the right moment. She, like me, was a long-standing social worker and a real hoot at times. She pulled her red-framed glasses down from her nose as she walked past. She was a buxom woman with dark hair that she wore in a bob, sometimes curly, sometimes straight. Most people in the office loved her.

"You talking to the plants again, Amber?" She put her arms around the edge of my cubicle and waited for my answer.

I gave her a haughty look. "It helps keep the plants alive. Josie is thriving. I just got a little slack with her watering."

The tight-lipped Lucy jutted out her ample hip and narrowed her eyes at me. "You need to find you a man. This plant is doing nothing for you right now."

She gestured in a humping motion, and I looked around to see if anyone had seen her. I shook my head, but we both giggled together. I could take a joke, and Lucy's facial expressions would have the whole office doubled over in laughter some days. Considering the type of cases we worked on, laughter was the best medicine to keep your mind off things.

I sighed heavily. "I agree with you. It's been a little while," I mumbled as I packed a few items into my purse.

Lucy looked at me with pitying eyes. She'd been happily married for the last five years. "You'll find you a good one. With all that long, blond hair and your tanned California skin, I'm sure there's one around the corner for you. You just need to put yourself out there a little more."

I glanced up at her. "Not so easy with my caseload right now, but I'll get there," I replied. At twenty-seven, I still felt like I was in my prime, dating-wise.

I stood up to leave. I didn't want to be late to meet Colt.

"I know! Let's go out for Friday night drinks. We haven't done that in a long time. Blow off some steam, you know." Lucy's eyes started to twinkle. She dramatically flicked one hand in the air.

I shook my head in feigned pain. "I can't. I have to help my neighbor Ruth with her planter boxes. I promised her I would."

Lucy rolled her eyes at me. "See? That's the reason you don't have a man. You're too busy helping all these other people. When are you going to help yourself, Amber? All these sexy curves are going to waste. Give them to me, and I'll show you what to do with them," Lucy said sassily as she slapped her hip. I watched it wobble.

Our boss, Donald, came past and spotted Lucy away from her cubicle. "Doing the rounds again, Lucy? You've been on lunch break for over an hour and a half. Time to get back to work."

"Yes, Donald dearest." She rolled her eyes at him as he walked back to his office. I laughed into my hand.

"Lucy, I have to go. I don't want to be late."

She gave me a curious look. "What case did you get?"

I slung my bag over my shoulder. "Colt Winters and his daughter Bella. The mother overdosed, and now Bella is staying with Colt's mother and father."

Lucy licked her lips and leaned closer to me, so only I could hear her. "Some of those prison boys are really good looking. I hope you at least get a hot criminal to look at."

HOPE STONE

I gave Lucy a light slap on the shoulder. "Lucy! I'm on a case. Shame on you."

She turned to walk away and looked back over her shoulder. "No, shame on you, honey, if you're not looking."

All you could do with Lucy was laugh sometimes. She was a wild one. I made my way to the glass doors and proceeded to my vehicle.

USP Atwater Penitentiary's conditions were diabolical. The prison needed a major overhaul. Many prisoners were committing suicide in their jail cells, and the death rates were steadily climbing.

"Our hands are tied. We can't do much about it. We're externally funded, and they won't give us the money to upgrade." That's what Warden Smith had told me on my last prison visit. I had wanted my brother, Hector, out of there as soon as possible.

My mind flashed back to my brother and when I'd last spoken to him on the prison phone. I'd said, "I'm going to get you out of here. You don't deserve to be in here. Those charges were bogus that you copped."

Hector, with his shaved head, put his hand to the glass, sliding his fingers down it. "Sister. I appreciate it, but we already appealed the other one, and it didn't go through."

One guard stood at the back of the room as I watched the clock. I had five minutes of talk time left that day. I splayed my fingers on the glass where his fingers were. "Little bro, this is what I do. Prison reform. You can't stay here. You're not safe. They just stabbed the prison teacher in here last year. The common room is too small. You're all bunched together. There are over a thousand inmates crammed in this place. There's bound to be a breakout of violence." My eyes bugged out of my head with fear and worry for my brother. I didn't dare tell Mom or Dad, or they would flip out. It was hard to conceal your brother's whereabouts for a whole year, though.

Hector looked back at me with hopelessness in his bright blue eyes. "Give up for a while. I'm just going to ride it out. I know what happened. My homeboy let me know what happened. It wasn't in my section."

I closed my eyes and grasped the steering wheel a little tighter as I thought back to the moment. It pained me greatly to see my brother like that. The lost look in his eyes hurt me. I vowed to do everything I could to reduce his sentence and protest about the conditions at USP.

As I contemplated my brother's case, I cleared my head to think about the reason for my current visit. Charlie "Colt" Winters and his baby girl, Bella. As far as I knew, Charlie was in a cell with one other man. I wondered how it was going for him. I guessed I was about to find out.

USP Atwater was right at the back of Merced in the middle of nowhere, a fifteen-minute drive and close to Castle Airport. I had plenty of time to gather my thoughts about the questions I had for Charlie as I drove there. I turned in where the sign said USP Atwater Penitentiary and found a spot to park. The parking lot was a little empty, and the main building was nothing to write home about. A single tier, sandy-colored building greeted me as I got out of the car. Dry, barren land surrounded the jail. I checked my purse for my official badge as I walked in the front door.

"Amber. Hey, how are you doing?" the warden welcomed me.

I smiled widely because it was important to stay in the good books with Warden Smith, so I got the visits I wanted and the access to achieve the prison outcomes I saw for the future of USP.

"Hey, Warden Smith. You're looking good today. How's your sweet wife doing?"

Warden Smith was an average looking man of normal height and a penchant for power. He ran a tight ship but, from all I knew, was a just and fair man. He smirked a little, but he couldn't hide the blush that came over his face. "You're just saying that. C'mon, who are you here to see?"

"I'm here to see Charlie Winters. It's about his daughter."

"Ah. Charlie. Mr. Outlaw. He's been behaving, and he's just about served his time. Six months to go on his sentence. He's a good inmate and an example for the others in here."

I nodded my head. That gave me some insight into the guy. "That's good to hear."

"So you know the drill. You have one hour with the inmate. I'll just do the standard check of your bag."

I opened my bag as I approached the backside of the jail. The warden scanned it and me. The scanning paddle that he had made a weird noise and then stopped.

"Okay, you're clear. He's waiting for you in the standard meeting room."

"Okay, thank you. I will see you on the way out."

"Indeed, you will." Warden Smith grinned.

A knot formed in the bottom of my throat. I always got a little nervous walking into the prison. The air changed when I walked in. A guard let me in the prison side and led me to the meeting room on the left. I saw the yellow stained door with a small window in it. He gestured me forward into the room.

"He's all yours," the guard said.

I smiled at him. "Thank you."

I stepped in, clutching my manila folder tightly. I struggled to maintain a neutral face as I scanned Charlie Winters up and down for good measure. His presence at the table took up a whole expanse of space. His eyes captivated me at first—ice blue pools of piercing coldness. I moistened my lips as I approached him. His sandy blond hair was neatly cropped on both sides, and his highlights on top stood out. His square, masculine jaw was clenched in position as he waited for me to speak first.

I held out my hand for him to shake. "Hi, I'm Amber Atwood, the social worker for your daughter, Bella."

He stood up, and I secretly admired his height and his impressive physical build. His large manly hand engulfed my small one as he gripped it lightly and let go. A lightning bolt of attraction surged through my system. I pulled out my chair and sat down as quickly as I could. His blue eyes twinkled, letting me know he was equally impressed by me.

"Great. I want to thank you for all you're doing for Bella. I've spoken to her on the phone, and she said you're a really nice lady."

I pulled out my case file from my purse and set it in front of me. "I'm so glad to hear that. She is a bright seven-year-old, and she's a pleasure to work with. She misses you."

Charlie looked down at his massive hands with guilt written all over him. "Yes. I know. I can't wait to get out of this hellhole. I just want to see my girl." The love for his daughter was evident in his voice.

"Charlie, would you like some water before we get started?" I reached out to the middle of the table where the water sat and attempted to pour into the plastic cups.

Charlie placed his hand over mine. "Let me. It's the least I can do—and call me Colt."

His beautiful, gleaming teeth made an appearance. I swear I started to swerve at the table from the sex appeal he oozed.

"Ah. Thank you. I appreciate it."

I gulped as a second knot formed in the pit of my stomach. His icy blue devils made the rounds over my body. I was modestly covered. I was wearing a blazer and a white top underneath. Opaque, because if it was see-through, prisoners might get ideas. I opted for black slacks, not too tight and not too baggy. Just right. It was hard to conceal my ample chest, though. It was sizable, and his eyes inadvertently moved there for a moment to rest. He watched me as he sipped his water. I let mine sit on the table.

"Shall we get started?" I realized I had my thighs squeezed together under the table in protest and loosened them a little.

"Yes. We can do that. How is my sweet Bella?"

His tenderness made my heart swell. "Bella is doing great. She is making strides at school and seems to be really enjoying it. She does ask a lot of questions about her mother. I do want to prepare you for that when you get out. I know it must be hard for you to talk about."

This man's forearms and biceps were like fully loaded cannons. I tried desperately not to look at them. Colt ran a hand through his blond hair and laced his fingers together. "I know. I mean, I'm going to have to talk to her some more. We talk on the phone about it. I don't want her to feel like she can't talk about her mother. I am just sucking it up. Obviously, Anna didn't cope well with me being locked up."

"It must have been upsetting for you to lose her like that."

"Yes. It was. I wish she could have thought about Bella more instead of herself. Thing is, I had no control over the situation. I couldn't be there to stop it from happening."

"Hey, it's not your fault. As you said, she wasn't coping."

"Well, no offense, but it is my fault that I ended up in here and Bella's without her father."

I straightened my jacket out a little and took a sip of water now. When I looked up, Colt's intense gaze was homed in on me. "So, Colt, any ideas for when you get out? I think having a solid exit plan will help you re-establish your relationship with Bella."

Colt fidgeted a little. "I agree. I have a plan. I want her to know that she's not going to lose me again and that she can rely on me."

"Good. Tell me more about Bella."

Colt's handsome face lit up as he began talking about her, how he'd been raising her to be a country girl, to climb trees and swim in the brook. After awhile, he paused and took another mouthful of water. "I used to read to her at night. I would rock her to sleep in my arms. She was so tiny. I've missed everything. She's grown up without me."

I watched as Colt dropped his head on top of his hands and slouched forward on the table. "Hey. It's not long to go now. Just take your time. It's going to be an adjustment when you get back home to her, but maybe your bond with the horses can be the entry point."

He lifted his head. "Maybe you're right. She used to help feed them every morning and talk to them. She's got a special way with them."

"See. That's a good start. How about you? How is your mental health here? I know the conditions aren't the best." I frowned as I looked him over.

"I'm not going to off myself if that's what you mean. But I've seen it. One of the guys in cell block D braided a bedsheet together, put in the grill above him, and tightened the knot. The guard found him, blue and stiff, hanging in his cell the next morning," he said matter-of-factly.

I winced when I heard this. I hated that anyone felt so low that they needed to take their own life, but who knew what demons these men held and what they were in prison for? My eyes averted to the clock behind Colt's head. We'd been talking for a good while, and our time together was almost up.

"That's terrible, Colt. Why do you think the rates of suicide are going up in here? Do they not have enough counseling sessions?"

"Nah. It's nothing to do with that. We're on top of one another. If you go out to the yard, there's no room to move.

That's why I ended up doing a lot of in-house activities to keep my mind alert. Going to classes. Signed up to cook. Just so I can get out of the cell."

"That's a great idea. You have new skills now. Are you going to live with Bella alone? Or will you keep your mother at your house? I want to make sure Bella is as comfortable as possible."

"Me too. I'll have to ask my little queen what she wants to do. Hopefully, she'll stay with me and live on the farm."

I noted a few things down on my sheets and drank the last of my water. "Colt, thank you for your time today. I see the time is almost up. I think you and your daughter will be just fine when you come out. I'll talk to you during our next visit about things you can do to ease her into the changes."

Colt brushed his eyes over my body one more time, sending a heat signal right to my sex. This man emanated primal masculinity. "Thank you again, Amber. You've set my mind at ease. I see that Bella is in good hands."

He shook my hand once again, and I relished the sensation of the soft pads of his fingers on mine. I signaled the guard for my exit.

I smiled courteously at him. "You're so welcome, Colt. I will let the Warden know so I can be added to the visiting list for next time."

I stood and collected my things.

COLT

Those big, brown eyes would make any man melt. The things I wanted to do with that sexy mouth of hers were an absolute sin. I let her walk out first, admiring the curve of her hips and her voluptuous backside as she sashayed out the prison meeting room. If she were one of the horses on my farm, I would want to rein her in. Her voice was soft and smooth like butter, easing my nerves. I knew my baby Bella was in safe hands, and that's all that mattered. Between Ms. Atwood and my mother, all would be well with her.

The prison guard left the door open and led me back to my cell. They always walked behind prisoners, I guessed, to avoid an attack. My heart dropped as I re-entered the hell-hole. My cellmate Errol was lying on his top bunk comfortably. Errol, a bank robber from Merced, was reading a book and had one foot crossed over the other. He was one hell of an eccentric character. He had a curled-up mustache and dark, slick hair. He was about the size of a toothpick and had an extra-pointy nose. He was as sly and as cunning as they came. You didn't get away with ten bank robberies for ten years without being that.

"Welcome back, cowboy. I just took a shit, so wrap your nose around that."

As soon as he said it, I felt the putrid aroma of jail feces perforate my nostrils. The problem with the conditions is that the cell only had one shitter for the two of us. We were boxed in together. No wonder murders and suicides were happening every other day.

"You bastard," I said slowly.

Errol looked over the top of his glasses and smiled. "Just for you, my friend."

"I could have done without your gift." The aroma was stinging my nostril hairs and making me sick. In all my four and a half years, I still wasn't used to it.

"Anything interesting happen?" Errol asked.

I let the smile coming from my lips lift my spirits. "Yeah, kind of."

Errol laid his book flat across his chest. "Do tell," he said in a deep voice.

"I got a decent social worker for Bella. She's really pretty, too. Blond, with big brown eyes."

"Forget the face." Errol tutted. He held his hands together as if he was holding watermelons. "What was the size of the tits? What did the ass look like? C'mon man, I've been in here for thirteen years. I need more to go on."

I shook my head. "You fucking pervert." I put my hand on the small wooden desk in front of me. I had a picture with Bella smiling taped to the wall. She was cuddled up in her mother's arms on the farm. I remembered that day so clearly.

"Daddy! Daddy! Can I ride Moonlight today? You promised. You said I could try."

The mortified look on Anna's face made me grin because I knew firsthand the bond that Bella shared with Moonlight. They both loved one another, and my instincts told me she wouldn't buck her off.

"Yes, but I'm going to be with you, leading you, okay?"

She'd clapped her little hands together and hugged my neck. "Yay! I'm happy today, Daddy. I'm happy!"

I came out of the memory, or rather Errol shook me out of it.

"Earth to farm boy. Tell me what she was like. I want to know!"

"Ah, she was sweet, real sweet. She promised to look after Bella for me. That's all I need her to do. I'm going home soon. I can't believe it," I confessed to Errol.

"You deserve it. You've served your time. Don't fuck it up and end up back here. I got another year to go. I'm trying to work on this appeal, but my lawyer is horseshit. That's why I'm reading." He held up the book to me, and I saw it was a legal handbook.

I frowned at him. "Backyard tactics? Think that will work?"

He lay back again on his bunk, gazing at the ceiling. "I mean, what the hell else am I supposed to do? I'm not going to just let it slide. This fuckface from cell block E is trying to scam me. We got a cigarette run going on, though. That's what I got running right now to keep myself amused."

I smirked lightly at him as I slipped into my bottom bunk. "You need me to get Austin involved?"

"Nah, I don't need any heavy hitters right now. I got it covered. I made a nice bit of pocket change. Two grand in the last two weeks. Not bad for a two-bit hustler, huh?" Errol chuckled weirdly.

"Not bad at all, Errol. You still got your stash from the main robbery you did? Did they ever find it?" I asked quietly.

I sank into the lumpy mattress, working to get comfortable. My large frame didn't fit so well on a single bed. My long legs hung off the end like a man in pants that are too short.

"Nah. Stupid cops. I got that stash waiting for me. I'm all

set. Just have to make it through the year and get the fuck out of here."

"How are you stashing that money? You better be careful in case they raid the cell."

Errol cackled. "My guy, I got players still in the game on the outside. They're stashing the money for me."

I rested my hands behind my head and quizzed him. "How do you know they will keep it for you?"

"Because I have too much on them. If they double-cross me, I will make sure they get ten years apiece. You hear me?"

"Loud and clear."

"What about you? Are you salty for taking the fall? You could have tattled on the Russians."

"If I wanted to be shot at point-blank range, that would be a viable option."

"You got a point there. They aren't too friendly. I've had a few run-ins with them myself. I managed to outsmart them, though. Not so bright, those Russians. Big oafs, really."

Errol and I had these enlightening prison conversations, and his bank robber stories kept me entertained. I even retained a few ideas from him. I would never forget when he gave me the rundown on prison etiquette when I first came in the cell. I smiled fondly at the memory.

"Number one, never hit the showers on Tuesday morning by yourself. You're bound to meet a big hunk of burning love in there. There's a standing arrangement," he had told me. *"Two, stay away from Frankie, Chase, Chester, and Raymond, the prison guards. Don't test them. Otherwise, they will test you with their batons. Three, get in good with the old-timers. They'll protect you if they choose to take you under their wing. Four, we got a cigarette run going, so if you need any, just let me know. I'm your man. All the rest, you learn on your own. Godspeed."*

His advice had never steered me wrong.

"It's all good. When I get out...I got plans for Bella and me. It's going to be a better life for us both."

I visualized the trails I had yet to take her on beyond the farm and stopping at the brooks she used to love swimming in. My mother, for all her great qualities, wasn't the one to do those things with Bella. She would teach her about growing crops and cooking. Bella would be free to roam, though. My mother didn't hold her kids to her. She didn't really need to. She knew all the mothers in the neighborhood and their kids. My mother was the quintessential farmer's wife.

I let my thoughts drift. I ran my mind's eye over the sensual-looking social worker's legs. She might have had those pants on, but they were tight enough for me to see what she was working with. I bit my lip as I pictured all the things I could do with her. I was at half-mast just thinking about it. I would be at full mast if I were back home in my own space. Hell, I would indulge that fantasy with her.

That was another thing about being in jail. You had absolutely no privacy whatsoever, so jerking off while your cellmate was right above you was a no-no.

Thing is, I'd seen her before. The more I envisaged her face, the more I realized it. She'd been talking to another young guy a few months back. A visit. I only caught a glimpse of that long, thick ponytail that reminded me of a horse's tail on the walk out.

A scuffling sound on the floor made me raise my head. I glanced sideways and saw that an envelope had been slid underneath the door. The bed creaked as I reached over and picked it up.

Errol didn't hear anything, and the incessant humming that he liked to do kept ringing through the cell. I opened the envelope and slid out the paper.

Meet me in the yard tomorrow. Frank.

The vindication I sought was about to be served up on a

platter. I hoped Frank would be able to point me in the right direction to Anna's dealer.

The news had come hard and fast in my fourth year. My mother was on the other end of the line. The warden came past the cell at noon on a stinking hot Merced day.

"You got a phone call, Winters. Your mother is on the line. You got half an hour for the call. C'mon and step out."

My mama never called. She just came on her regularly scheduled days like clockwork. She always had the same hairstyle: a shaggy salt and pepper bob with bangs that she got cut at the same place all the time. She never complained. My mother was the strong but silent type. She was tall, wispy, and strong. I guessed that's where I got my height from because Pops was small, wiry, and athletic. They were an odd couple, but they sure as hell knew how to run an abundant farm.

As I walked out, a strange sensation came over me. When I picked up the payphone on the wall, I knew why. I had the phone cord linked around my fingers. Her weeping made it hard for me to talk to her. I hated the thought of my mama in pain. She'd toiled long and hard all her life, and taking over the farm was the least I could do to ease the burden.

"Mama. What's wrong? Quit crying and tell me."

"Anna. It's Anna." She could barely get the words out as the ugly cries filtered through the other end of the line. "She's gone."

My mouth dropped open, and I blinked rapidly, not sure of what I'd just heard. "Come again? Who's gone? What do you mean, Anna's gone?"

"She—she couldn't do it anymore, I guess, son. She overdosed on heroin. I found her with a needle in her arm. Bella was there. I made sure she didn't see it. I promise you. She didn't see it. God, Colt, it was awful."

I slumped down the wall. "No. You're lying. Tell me you're lying. Bella...Anna. No, Mama."

"Son, I'm so sorry." My mother's distress and pain vibrated in every syllable that rolled off her tongue.

"What am I going to do?" My face screwed up in agony, and anger ripped through me in a million different ways. My heart broke like shattered glass hitting the floor.

"I have to go. I have to pick Bella up from school. I will see you on Tuesday, and we can talk more then. The police are coming, too. She just couldn't live without you. You were her anchor."

"Mama. Please. Stay on the line. Mama. How did she? When did she do this?"

"I didn't tell you. I thought it best. She was trying to get clean. She tried. She really did."

Anger, despair, rage, and an acute sense of grief took me over as my mama changed her tone and delivered the final blows. But I knew. I just didn't want to admit it. I didn't want to ask. The sunken black eyes were evident every time Anna came to visit. I saw it in her visible collarbone jutting out on both sides and her shaky, bony fingers. I was just happy to see her and to know that someone was by Bella's side. Maybe if I'd said something, she could have gotten help. I could have saved her. But I didn't. I just smiled at her through the perspex glass and gave her a kiss goodbye every time she came. I let her die.

I held on to that in my heart for a long time.

Now I had the chance to set the record straight, once and for all. I had a mission of vengeance for a worthy cause.

AMBER

I struggled to open my car door when I left the prison. I walked out into the Merced sun, dazed and confused about what I'd just witnessed. The lump in my throat was firmly lodged as I threw my paperwork and purse onto the front seat. Oh hubba, hubba what a hunk of a man. He belonged in a magazine with that chiseled jaw and those delicious toned, sinewy arms. Lucy had been right. If she only knew how much.

I hoped the flush of hot lust didn't show on my face too much when I met him. I made every attempt to keep everything professional. Even the way his lips moved as he talked turned me on. The whole fifteen-minute car ride back to the office, all I saw was those iceberg-blue eyes. From the way his eyes mowed me down, I figured the feelings of attraction were mutual. Then again, the guy had been cooped up with men for the last four and a half years.

I parked in my usual spot. I fluffed my hair and took a tissue to my face and between my boobs to wipe the sweat away. Some of the heat, however, didn't just come from the sun. I sauntered into the office, welcoming the cool of the air conditioning. I snuck into my desk. I didn't want Lucy to hound me about the visit. I feared I would give myself away if she saw my face.

I shuffled and played with the paperwork on my desk for way too long. I had a pile of reports to check in with. First, I needed some tea to calm my racing heart down. Colt Winters. Amber Winters. It had a nice ring to it. I shook off the thought of last names and headed to the break room kitchen. I had my phone with me. I glanced at it briefly as it went off with a text. It was my little brother, Hector. What did he want?

I hummed joyfully to myself and made a cup of instant coffee. That prison visit had me in the right mood. I finished pouring my coffee and snuck a few cookies from the staff jar. I bit into the chocolatey goodness and read my text.

Call me. I have something urgent to tell you.

A troubled frown came over my face. Uh-oh. I put my two hands on either side of the counter and hung my head a little. My brother Hector was only twenty-five years old and had already served one year at USP Atwater for assault and armed robbery. Luckily, he took a plea bargain to reduce his sentence. He broke the code and snitched on a couple of people, but he did the right thing in my mind. He survived. The memory of me picking him up from Atwater flashed through my mind.

The first thing I told him was, "Stay out of trouble. You've done your time now. You're on twelve months probation and two hundred hours of community service. You have to keep your nose clean."

He'd given me a sloppy kiss on the side of my face and hugged me. I'd wiped it off in disgust. "Love you, Amber. Thanks for holding it down."

"You're welcome, and I'm so glad you're home. I love you." My heart felt lighter now that he was home, but given the text message I'd just received, it was starting to shrink again.

I took my cup of coffee and cookies out back, away from prying eyes and ears.

"Hi," I said cagily.

I sat down on the backstep. The sunshine hit the left side of my face, making me squint. I placed my coffee beside me, dunked my cookie in the hot liquid, and bit into it. I tried to keep my crunching away from the phone.

"Hey," Hector replied flatly.

"What's wrong, baby bro? You sound down." A large truck rumbled past, and I waited to hear his answer after it passed.

"I got a situation," he replied warily.

My back became erect as I honed my ears to listen. "What kind of trouble are you talking about, Hector?"

He released a large breath into the phone. "The Las Balas crew. Apparently, there's a hit out on me. They're trying to pin me for a prison debt. I'm in big shit, Amber. I need some help."

Cool, calm, and collected is how I responded with clients when they presented their problems to me. After all, I was a social worker and was used to dissecting people's lives without judgment, putting the pieces of the puzzles back together. I held the phone away from my face and stared at it blankly.

"Hector. Are you serious? How do you know the threat came from Las Balas?" I replied evenly.

"It's from them. A few of the guys I used to run with told me over beers. They wanted to warn me about it. I'm telling you because I may need to relocate until I figure it out."

"Why should you run? What the hell are they talking about? A prison debt?" I twisted my head around to make sure no one was outside smoking and might hear me.

"Don't worry about it."

"Hector! You called me, remember? You're my only

brother. Of course I'm worried about it. You've been doing so good," I said.

"Apparently not good enough for Las Balas. They're looking for some money that was given to me from the robbery. The cops took it, so of course, I don't have it. There's no way I can pay it back," he replied desperately.

"How much is it, Hector?" My voice trembled as I lifted my coffee to my mouth. I burned my lip from misjudging the heat of it and winced. "Shit!"

"You all right?" Hector asked in a concerned voice.

"Yeah. I just burnt my lip with the coffee," I grumbled.

"Two hundred thousand. Sorry to call you with my bullshit. I'm freaking out a little bit. Las Balas aren't a crew I want bad blood with," Hector said apprehensively. "I know you're connected. You know, in the prison system. I thought—"

I cut him off. "You thought what?"

"I don't know. That you would know somebody on the inside to help out or have a contact. Something. I'm fresh out of ideas here."

I dunked the second half of my cookie in the coffee and tried to let my mind go someplace else. The Merced heat was starting to agitate me along with Hector. "Leave me with it, and I'll see what I can do."

"Hey. Thanks, Amber. 'Preciate it," Hector groveled.

"Okay. I have to get back to work, okay? Give me a couple of days, and we'll come up with a plan."

That's what I did—came up with plans for everyone else other than myself. I had no real complaints, just every now and then it wore me down. I grimaced as I rose from the concrete step. As I looked at the clock, I noted I only had a couple of hours to go, then I could retire to my safe haven with a glass of red. The remainder of my workday passed by quickly, and the pile of paperwork on my desk now looked half the size. I had my headphones on most of the time to concentrate on my cases. When I dragged my head up, it was time to go home.

As I strode out to my car with my bundle of cases to look through, I thought of my brother and me in simpler times. The fun we used to have. We would build fortresses in our backyard, and he would chase me, playing tag. Now he was fresh out of prison with a hit on him.

I rode home to the little house that I'd bought five years ago. It was set back from the main strip of Merced, and I loved it. My luscious green hanging plants welcomed me as I reached my front steps. I tapped them, and they swung silently. I loved my porch, where I could bask in the iconic California sunsets on gorgeous nights like tonight. The skyline looked like fresh cantaloupe had been spread across it. I didn't want to miss it, so I hurried to drop my bags and pour myself a glass of wine.

I took one sip and headed to the shower to wash away the day. Colt's sinewy, thick arms swirled into the steam as a memory while I loofahed myself clean. What I wouldn't do to have those arms around me in the shower. It sent tingles all through my body just thinking about it.

I toweled off and set up some cheese and crackers to go with my wine. My case paperwork was waiting where I'd dropped it off on the porch. I took another delicious sip of red wine as I marveled at the intense changes in the sunset. I took a seat, opened my manilla folder, and re-read the case notes from Colt's file. Sexy Colt. He was a farmer who grew his own produce. It's not like I hadn't seen the file before. It just took on new meaning now that I'd met him. He was also a former member of the Outlaw Souls. I sliced some cheese on my plate and laid it on top of my water crackers. I re-read that bit again. Outlaw Souls.

An epiphany struck. That's it! Colt was the connection I

needed for Hector. Colt from the Outlaw Souls. From what I knew, they were huge rivals of Las Balas. Colt was part of the Merced chapter and surely would be able to offer a solution. The problem was that my next visit with him wasn't until next month. Prisoners typically got four hours of visit time a month, and I'd already taken up one hour of his time. It was worth a shot, though. I would see if I could pull some strings since the warden liked me so much.

I scribbled down on my notepad the reminder for a scheduled visit to see Bella. I wanted her to be ready for Colt's return. I worked late into the night, as always. A social worker's notes are never complete. There were so many children and people I wanted to save, but the thing is, I couldn't reach them all. By the time I carried myself off to bed, it was well after ten.

The next morning I woke up at eight o'clock. I wiped the sleep out of my eyes. Hector was the first thought that came to my mind. I rolled over from the comfort of my blanket, unclipping my phone from the charger. I lay on my back and punched in my little brother's number.

"Hey, little brother," I said sleepily.

"How many times have I asked you not to call me that? I'm a grown man. Not your little brother," he grumbled.

"I know that. To me, though, you're the one I used to boss around when we were making fortresses in the backyard," I added in a melancholy tone.

"I remember that, and you're still telling me what to do. Nothing's changed."

"Listen. I have an idea of what to do about your situation. I'm not saying don't leave town. That might be a good idea. But I know an inmate at USP that's part of the Outlaw Souls. He may have some insight into what to do. No guarantees, but it's a start."

"You would do that? Outlaw Souls are a direct enemy to

Las Balas, so that would help a lot. I have to do something. I am taking off, though."

"Where are you headed? Can I reach you?" I sat up in bed and threw the blanket back. It was time to get up.

"Eventually. I don't want you connected to me. If they find out you're my sister, then you're dead meat. I can't do that to you. I will send word when I get going. I'm heading to San Fran."

"Can't you just tell me now?" I steamed.

"No." Hector had put his metaphorical foot down.

Flustered, I blew my thick hair out of my face and looked in the mirror. My curves were getting a little out of control. I blamed it on the stress of the job.

"Okay. Do what you have to do and stay safe. You're going to need to contact me somehow. I will have information for you," I said.

"I know. Like I said, it will only be a couple of days. I'm just going to let the heat die down a little," Hector argued.

"Okay. Well, let me get off the phone and organize this prison visit." I surrendered because there was not much I could do if he wouldn't listen to reason. I moved to the coffee pot in the kitchen.

"Great. See you when I'm looking at you. Take care, Amber."

"Bye." I hung up the phone and waited for my coffee to get ready. I made a call to USP and got the switchboard.

"Hello. Can I please be put through to Warden Smith? My name is Amber Atwood. I'm from the Human Services Agency in Merced."

"One moment, please, and I will see if he is available to speak with you."

I shifted my weight from one leg to the other as I anticipated his voice.

"Hi, Amber. I didn't expect a call from you so soon. What

can I do for you?" Warden Smith answered with anticipation. I could literally hear his lips smacking together.

"Hi, Warden Smith. I know this is an abnormal request, but I had a visit with Colt Winters recently." I paused as I concocted the lie. "I forgot a few details from his file, and something has come up with his daughter. I need to speak to him right away. Do you think I can arrange a visit with him? I don't want his visiting hours to be affected, though. This is a special visit."

The warden let the silence hang thickly in the air for a moment. "We normally don't allow that, but Colt is a model citizen, and I'm a reasonable man. Plus, it's you that's asking. For anyone else, I wouldn't, but I will get the message to him and come back to you with a time and date."

"Great. Thank you!" Relief flooded through my body with the news.

Where there's a will, there's a way.

COLT

Raymond was on duty, stalking the prison halls. Raymond was a guard I'd been warned about beforehand. This man had an ego the size of a mountain and the anger of a pit bull. Once his jaws locked down on you, there was no telling what damage he could do. His chubby fingers rested on his slick black baton. The crunch of his polished black boots could be heard a mile away. The other guards' boots I couldn't hear, but Raymond's I could. It sounded like he had steel taps on the bottom of them. I never bothered to look at the time some days, but now, since I was getting out, I tended to glance at it a little more.

Errol was being disgusting and clipping his nails, dangling his feet over his bunk bed. Raymond peeped in the cell with his beady yellowish eyes. His overgrown belly rubbed against the cell bars.

"Colt. Got a message for you. Get over here," Raymond commanded.

I stretched my height up from the wonky chair I was sitting in and crossed over to him. I recoiled slightly. His breath stank like a thousand deaths. "What's the message?"

"Social worker is coming to visit tomorrow," he said with a disgusted look on his rotund face. His bald head glistened as he spoke, and I focused my eyes on the shine from the light.

"Okay. Great. What time is she coming?" I asked.

"She's coming when she is, boy. I'll come and get you. I'm on duty, so it's your lucky day tomorrow. Don't be getting fresh with me, or I will send you to solitary confinement."

I said nothing and eased back to the desk. I knew who to talk back to and who not to talk back to. Raymond waited, poised for the verbal retaliation. When he was satisfied that there would be none, he moved on with his noisy boots.

Errol gave me a knowing stare from the top bunk, swinging his legs. Once Raymond was out of earshot, he said, "That guy needs a royal ass-kicking. Someone needs to put out a jail hit on him. Could make it so that he accidentally slips and falls in the laundry room. Death by laundry liquid. What you think?"

I belly laughed so hard I had to cover my mouth. I was lucky enough to have a great cellmate for my five-year stay in the hellhole hotel. "Sounds like a winning plan to me. Let's execute."

Errol jumped down to sit beside me on the chair. "You want me to torture you in spades again? I'm bored."

"Nah. I have to meet somebody in the yard. There's some unfinished business I have to take care of."

"Unfinished business," Errol repeated as he slid the playing cards out of the deck and shuffled. "Anything to do with Anna?"

Shocked, I stared hard at Errol. "How'd you know?"

"Something told me you're not the type of man to let something like that slide." He pointed to the picture of Bella and Anna on the wall.

I cracked my knuckles in silent rage. "You're not wrong. They killed my woman and left Bella with no mother."

Errol tapped me on the back with his long spindly fingers. "Don't end up back here in the process. I'm rooting for you. I want to sit talking to you when I get out of here. Do you need back-up on anything? Cover?"

I rubbed my fingers a few times. "No. I'm fine. The old-timers will have my back." Doom settled in my voice nonetheless.

"Okay." Errol nodded. "You got a real treat for the day. Two outings. You get to see that pretty social worker again. Blondie."

I tried to hide the smile, but the blood pumped through all my body parts when I thought about running my hands through her hair and overtaking her pretty mouth. I wondered how many times I could make her moan.

"Yeah. I get to see her. I don't know what she wants, though. I hope everything is okay with Bella. I mean, why else does she need to see me?" I asked, secretly hoping it was because she was feeling me.

"Beats me, farm boy. Wait and see, I guess," Errol responded dismissively.

The yard bell rang, and I stood up, waiting for the cell to unlock. The customary click came. Another prison guard came to let us out. Thankfully, it wasn't Raymond. I walked to the yard and, like always, breathed the limited oxygen into my lungs. I ran my eyes over the scene. No one was at the weight bench today. A few guys gathered around on one side, though. One of the prison inmates was performing. Singing. His melodic tones floated all the way over to me. I nodded my head. The guy had some pipes. He wasn't half bad.

Austin and another beefy dude with full tattoo sleeves were sitting on top of one of the benches. His face held the look of a man you wouldn't want to mess with. His eyes were as cold as steel. His lips were held in a thin line. His face was clean-shaven, and he had a tattoo on the side of his thick neck. Heavy eyelids gave one of his eyes a slanted appearance.

"Hey. Colt, right?" he posed.

"Yep. That's me," I responded.

Frank slid his eyes both ways to look at the guard. His eyes were on the group crowded around the yard singer of the day. Austin sat serenely next to him and started humming. Frank nodded.

"All right. Austin tells me you're good people. Any friend of Austin's is a friend of mine. So what's the score?" Frank asked.

"Thanks. Look, I need some help. My girlfriend died from an overdose, and I know for a fact that a Las Balas member sold her the drugs. Can you sew that situation up for me?"

Frank's cold eyes looked through me. "I heard about it through the grapevine. I'm sorry for your loss. You're Outlaw family, too. I've been the eyes and ears for the crew for a long time now. We'll put a stop to this sucker. Give me a little time, and I'll send out word about it." He gazed away from me as he spoke.

"Thanks. I appreciate it. What do I owe you?" I asked pensively.

"Nothing at all. That's what we Outlaws do. We stand for the brotherhood of all our riders. You got a daughter. I have one, too. We have to protect them from street slime." Frank spat on the ground, and it landed two feet away from him.

I nodded with respect. "Agree. Respect the code. Check you later."

"Good. Peace, brother." Frank saluted, and I moved around the yard to converse with the other inmates.

As time passed and the guards let us back to our cells, I visualized my exit and how I planned to come back into society. Could I go back to the Outlaw Souls? Or would I have to straighten up and fly right? Maybe I would just work on the

HOPE STONE

farm and leave the rest alone. As sleep called me, I floated off to think about the sensual social worker and what I had to look forward to.

In my dream, she entered the meeting room.

"Colt, I came to see you. When I saw you last time, I knew I had to come back. I find you to be irresistible. I have to be with you." She ripped open her white collar shirt and revealed her ample breasts. She slid down her skirt and crawled across the desk to meet me, sitting in my lap.

I woke up sweaty, embarrassed, and hard from the fantasy.

Errol was brushing his teeth and spitting out the contents in the sink. I could smell the minty freshness of the toothpaste. Not many odors got away from my nose due to the coziness of the cell. I stretched my tight muscles and yawned.

"Hey, farmer. You better do what I'm doing. Aren't you seeing that social worker soon?"

Dazed and confused from my slumber, I replied slowly. "Yeah. Ought to be. I don't know what time, though. That prick Raymond wouldn't tell me."

"You better be up for shower time before she gets here. She doesn't want to mix with a stinky farmhand," Errol replied in amusement. He'd used some water and a little gel to slick back his hair and twirl the ends of his mustache. He was one of the stranger characters I'd met in the jail, but I was grateful I was in the cell with him and not some of these other freaks.

"Shut up. I'll be ready," I countered.

As soon as it was mentioned, Raymond's click-clacking boots came down the corridor to our cell. "Colt. Shower time is now if you're going to go. Be ready. Twenty minutes later, you have a meeting."

His mustardy stained teeth made me flinch. Someone should have alerted him to his mouth hygiene. Raymond clicked the cell open and tapped his slick black baton as

46

normal. A veiled threat. I eyed him closely and sloped away from him and out of the cell. My towel was hung over my shoulder as he walked behind me to the showers.

Every time I came to the showers, I cased the shower block, looking both ways like when crossing the road. In the shower was the time when prisoners got stabbed with homemade shanks designed to take one another out at their most vulnerable moments. My muscles were coiled like a cobra, ready to fight should I need to. Today, the showers were free, and no one was in them. I lathered up and let the hot water hit my skin. I opened my mouth and let the water trickle in. My bunched-up muscles relaxed a little but not much.

It took three minutes flat for me to wash from top to bottom and dress in the sandy brown uniforms of USP. I peered at myself in the mirror, clenching and unclenching my jaw at the small mirror sink. Pretty good for being in jail for close to five years. I decided to leave the light stubble on. Ladies liked a little two o'clock shadow from what I knew. Amber's sweet California smile made me suck in a breath as I thought about what type of man she might like.

"Hey, pretty boy. Are you keeping out of trouble?" I heard a teasing voice come from the left. I retracted my fingers to form a fist on each side. I turned to the voice, ready to take down whoever was speaking.

"Whoa, player. It's not that serious. It's just me," Dante, an African American with dreads, pleaded, holding up his palms. Immediately, I released my hands as he hung his towel, ready to shower.

"You never know. You know how it is, Dante."

"I sure do. I'm not wrangling with you, though. That's for sure," he claimed, giving me the once-over.

"How you holding up?" I asked him as I brushed my teeth.

"Man. I'm all right. Got my fill here. A day in jail is longer

HOPE STONE

than anybody should be in here. I have six days to go, and then I'm out. I have to get a new hustle," Dante responded in frustration.

"You and me both. I got six months of torture to go," I replied.

"Okay. Good. No offense, but I hope I never see you again." Like me, Dante took a quick shower and towel-dried fast.

I laughed. "Agreed. See you later, man," I said and waited for the guard to return so I could head back to the cell.

Raymond gave me a look over as he returned, as promised, twenty minutes later.

"Okay. Time to go see your mistress." Raymond sneered. "I tell you what, I wouldn't mind knocking her down. She has a nice rack, huh?"

I felt every part of my body tense with the urge to crack this guy's skull open. I wrangled with myself to keep my face neutral. "I guess if that's what you like."

I walked in front and towards the daylight of the prison meeting rooms.

Raymond replied, "Oh, what, do you like men? Do you like some of these boys in here? I can line you up with one if you like." His hot, rancid breath hit the side of my neck. Again, I didn't fold.

"Nope. I only like women." I waited at the locked door for him to open it.

"Good to hear, prisoner. I wouldn't want you to become a prison bitch," he threatened.

He clicked the alarm code to exit the prison and step into the meeting room. Through the window, I could see Amber looking around aimlessly. My body wanted to fly in the room and get as far away from Raymond as possible. I made a mental note to ask Frank if somebody could take him out as well.

48

Amber looked like an angel. Her face was soft, with pretty pale lip gloss and a smile. Just what I needed to brighten my existence. Her unruly, thick blond hair made me want to run my hands through it. Her worried expression made me nervous, however.

Raymond opened the door and waved to Amber with a grin. Amber apparently caught on, as well. She gave him a smile that didn't reach her eyes.

"One hour only," he warned. I didn't reply.

"Hi, Amber." I smiled at her, grateful the slimy man had left us alone.

She returned the smile. "Hi, Colt. Nice to see you again. Please, take a seat." She gestured to the chair.

"Thanks. You're back sooner than I expected. Please tell me that there's nothing wrong with my daughter," I begged.

Her face soothed me as her frown flattened. "No, not at all."

She licked her beautiful lips, and I shifted my erection. She was a massive turn-on. I wanted her so badly. "Okay. What is it, then?"

"I—I have a problem. It's connected to my little brother. I need some help." She lowered her voice and looked to the back of the guard's head outside the door.

"All right." I leaned in and matched her lowered tone. "Go ahead. I'll see what I can do to help."

"Hector's a good kid. He really is. He's twenty-five, and he got mixed up in the wrong situation with a motorcycle gang called Las Balas. I thought since you have—or did have— dealings with the Outlaw Souls, you might be able to help?" Her soulful caramel eyes made me want to hold her.

"Still have dealings with. They are my brothers. Las Balas are a nasty bunch of fuckheads. What's the problem? I'm sure I can help. Tell me."

"Hector has a hit out on him. He's on the run and said he

would call me in a couple of days. The amount is more than I can handle. It's a two hundred thousand dollar debt from an armed robbery gone wrong. The police department seized the stolen funds. I don't know what to do," she confessed, her hands going to her temples as she brushed back the thickness of her hair.

I took her hands as if it was the most natural thing in the world and slid my thumb across her skin to calm her. I saw the tears welling in her eyes as she spoke.

"Don't worry. I'm pretty sure I can help with this. I have connections here that will be able to let me know what's what. Good thing he's out of town. The last time Las Balas put a hit out, they shot the guy within forty-eight hours," I said matter-of-factly. I watched as her face twisted in horror. "I didn't mean to scare you. I just think it's good that he left town until it's cleared up. Are you okay? Do they know about you?"

I watched the cadence of her breath rise and fall. I could tell the situation had her panicked.

"I mean, I don't know. I don't think so. What can you do? What would you do?" she pleaded.

"Well, first off, I have my connections, as I said. I can't reveal my sources, but I can talk to them and see if they can work out a game plan. How the hell did he become involved with Las Balas?"

"I don't know. Just, you know, being a stupid, reckless kid. He didn't know the guy he robbed was a gang member with connections, I guess. He would never tell me the full story, so I'm just guessing." She spoke fast, and her words tumbled out. I eyed her with concern as she tucked stray tendrils of her golden hair behind her ear. She lit up the whole room, including me. I didn't like seeing her upset.

"I'm sorry you're going through that. Can't be easy," I sympathized.

"Please. You're going through the death of your girlfriend and being in prison for five years. I saw from your file that you covered for someone. That's what the case looks like." She narrowed her eyes at me.

"I mean. I ain't no snitch. Are you always so selfless?" I changed the subject.

She gazed at her hands for a moment. "Part of my job, I guess."

"Who takes care of you?" I asked softly, meeting her eyes with mine.

"I guess I take care of myself. I'm good."

"Are you?" I challenged her.

She lifted her head backward, so her swan-like neck was exposed. I wanted to run my fingers along with my tongue down it. I wanted to make her moan and feel good, but this was neither the time nor the place.

"I'll be okay, Colt. If you could, please do what you can and let me know as soon as possible. Do you have my card?" she asked.

"Yep. I have it. I will organize to call you as soon as I work out a plan. We'll get your brother out of it. Anything to get rid of those bastards," I replied angrily.

"Thank you."

It seemed like I wouldn't need an excuse to see the pretty social worker. Now I had a wide-open link to her.

AMBER

I left the prison with a sliver of hope. Just a little light at the end of the tunnel. First, Colt had to get to his people and see what they could do. Maybe, and only maybe, would I be able to help Hector.

I drove straight to see Bella from the prison. I wasn't due at the office until the afternoon. As soon as I drove along the dusty track to the house, my heart lifted. This felt like another part of Merced with the fresh California country air and luscious evergreen trees in plentitude. On Colt's property, there was a stream running along the backside.

I pulled up and got out. The house was long and a single story. It was built in a triangular shape with high wood ceilings. From the front, it looked like an all-American summerhouse with a wraparound porch. I was a sucker for porches. I loved the place, and it was a far cry from the inner city walkups in Merced that smelled like pee from tenants pissing in the hall. Many of the places I had to visit on my rounds for social work had roaches crawling around. Some of the cases were super sad and broke my heart. I'd learned to cope over the years, but I never really found a way to numb it out totally.

I rapped my knuckles on the door a few times and waited. I heard an older lady's gravely voice cry out down the hall, "Who is it? I'll be right there. Is that you, Amber?"

The pitter-patter of little feet followed. "Amber. Amber! She's here, Grandma!"

My heart burst open with love as a bright young girl with chestnut pigtails and yellow ribbons opened the door. Bella's curly pigtails bounced as she turned her face to her grandma. Colt's mother, Cheryl, wiped her hands on a tea towel.

"Excuse my hands, sweetheart. I was baking some chocolate chip cookies before you came. Come on in. You're just in time to have some." The pleasant, slim, silver-haired lady beckoned me through the hallway to the kitchen.

As I walked through, I admired the sense of family togetherness. Pictures of Colt in his younger years on horses were on the shelves along with photos of all of them together, picking in the fields. There was one of Colt swimming in a river, and even then, he looked fit and even more handsome. It must be hard to see their only child imprisoned.

"Guess what, Ms. Atwood? I got a gold star in school today. I helped my friend Mason lift something. I got the award for being helpful," Bella beamed proudly.

Cheryl chuckled and gazed out the large kitchen window. "You sure did, and you sure are helpful around the house. Could you do Grandma a favor and check the mail for me? I think I left a letter or two in there from yesterday. You know, my memory is kind of foggy."

"Silly Grandma," Bella giggled. "I will check. Save some cookies for me!" She stampeded off to the front, giving us some time to talk.

Cheryl's eyes were sparkly, bright, and kind. She was in

her late sixties from what Colt had told me. All the farm work made her a strong and wily older lady.

"She's doing great, little Bella. Growing every day. She misses her Mama. She sometimes cries at night. I go in and sit with her. Usually, a glass of milk and a lullaby puts her back to sleep. It was such a shame about her mother. I wish I hadn't found her like that. Better me than Bella, though. How is my boy?"

"That must have been terrible. I hope you're okay now. Colt is doing great. He looks healthy, and he sends his love. Are you ready for him to come back here?"

"Funny, but I've come to love it here again. It's been a great sacrifice, but now I don't see it that way. The workers come and go. It keeps me out of trouble, and I get to play a part in Bella growing up. I won't know what to do with myself when I go home," she commiserated as she looked out of the big kitchen window.

I gave her a winning smile. "Mrs. Winters, you are doing a fine job. I was going to ask since it will be a transition for Bella. I would recommend that you stay here, maybe for another week. Just so that Colt can get acclimatized to being back home and with the changes on the farm."

She nodded and slid two cookies in front of me. "Would you like a cup of Joe?"

"No. I already had one before I left home. If I drink another, I will be bouncing off the walls."

She flung the tea towel over her shoulder. "I know what you mean. I much prefer a cup of tea any day. I do think that's a good idea to be here with Colt. He hasn't seen Bella much at all. Prison timing and all that. He doesn't even know what she's like day to day. It's going to be interesting for all of us."

I nodded. "I'm sure Colt will slip right back into things," I said cheerfully.

"I don't know. I think young Bella is going to teach him a thing or two about how things work around here," she said.

I giggled. "I'm sure she will. Do you think Colt will be able to cope with the changes here? Is there anything new at the farm I should inform him about?"

She sipped from her teacup, gazing out the window wistfully. "No. He will be just fine. There's nothing too crazy going on here. Colt knows this land like the back of his hand. He ought to. He sowed the crops by hand some years when our machinery broke down."

Colt placing his hands in the soil and bringing something to life sent a distinct shiver of desire down my spine. "Wow. He's a real man's man, isn't he?"

"My boy is a cowboy, through and through." She smiled. "He loves those horses. You should come with me to the stables, and I'll show you them."

Her warmth made me feel all gooey inside. Mrs. Winters was a mother anyone would love to have. I couldn't help but feel at ease in Cheryl's presence. I dipped my eyes to my purse, checking the time on my watch. I still had another half hour.

Cheryl caught my glance and flicked her hand at me. "Don't worry, they won't miss you so much. Have a little time to yourself, dear. You do a lot in your profession. It must be hard what you do, with all the stories I hear."

"It can be rough some days, but it's rewarding, too. I mean, I get to work with beautiful little girls like Bella."

Speaking of the bright, bubbly little girl, she came rushing toward us as we stepped outside.

"Hey, you guys! Grandma, there wasn't any mail. I checked and checked again."

The corner of Cheryl's mouth lifted into a wry smile. "Oh, thank you anyway, baby, for taking a look."

Bella grabbed on to her grandma's hand. I still had a job to do, so I asked Bella some questions as we trudged along the path.

"So, Bella, are you ready for your daddy to come home?"

She nodded her head enthusiastically. "I can't wait. I want to tell him about my riding. I can ride Moonlight by myself. She loves me. Her coat is so shiny. And I look after all the chickens! I collect all the eggs." A few chickens came gathering around Bella as if on cue as we closed in on the barn.

"They lay their eggs in the barn. We don't cage them up. We want all animals to be free here!" She twirled around.

I nodded, impressed. "Free-range eggs. Very nice."

Cheryl looked at me as if she'd forgotten something. "Would you like to take some fresh eggs with you, dear? We have plenty."

I smiled. "If you can spare some eggs, I will take them off your hands."

"Yes. Of course we can." Cheryl patted my arm in reassurance.

I turned to Bella. "Do you love the horse as much as your father does?"

"Yes. He must be missing Moonlight. She's his favorite. The dark one. I like Moonlight, too. 'Cept she can be temperamental. I hope she remembers him. If she doesn't like people, she will just buck them off."

The lightness of her childlike spirit made me smile. I listened to the rustling of the wind through the trees. I noted the workers coming to and fro from another shed at the back of the property. It prompted me to ask the question, "How are the workers getting on out here without Colt?"

"They all used to work for me. Well, all of them except three new ones. We passed the farming business down to Colt. So it's like riding a bike for me and Clive. We stepped right back into our old roles."

Cheryl walked with her hands clasped behind her back.

We approached a red timber barn full of hay. The smell of horse manure and feed passed my nostrils. Bella ran ahead to the horses, all of which were standing tall behind stable doors made from wood. The first head I saw was the majestic Moonlight. She bowed her head to us, flaring out her nostrils.

My mouth opened wide. I felt like I was in the presence of royalty. Her coat shone black as night with parts of it reflecting from the sunlight. Her beautiful, huge eyes watched, checking me out. Cheryl gave me an encouraging push toward her.

"It's okay. She sorts out who is who here. Play nice, and she will play nice with you."

Tentatively, I stepped forward. Moonlight quietened, and I reached out my hand, my heart pounding in my chest. I didn't want her to bite me. I stroked her nose, and she lowered her head and nuzzled my neck. Startled, I jumped back. Moonlight reared her head up, and she appeared to be just as scared as me. Maybe horses are mirrors to us. I didn't know.

"Easy now. She will be fine. She likes you. That's why she did that. Take it as a fine compliment from her. She's been known to give the workers a nip or two. She lets us know who to fire and who to keep."

"Wow. She is something truly special."

"We think so."

"Grandma! Grandma! Can I feed them?" Bella pleaded.

"Sure you can. Go right ahead."

Bella went to a haystack on the side, and I watched as she lifted the golden straw into the stables of the Palomino horses. She was beyond her years.

I was tired, just watching her. "Where does she get her energy? I mean, she's like a little adult."

"That she is. She's doing great in school, by the way. Gets along with all the kids. They come here and run around. They never want to leave. But why would you?" Cheryl raised her hands as she turned around the stable.

I giggled a little as the chickens clucked near my feet, and the horses kept watch. It reminded me of a scene out of Babe. She was absolutely right. "Can I ask you another question?"

"Go ahead, shoot."

"Think Colt can keep it together when he gets out?" I wiped the little bit of sweat on my face. It must have been from being enclosed in the barn.

"He can. He just got caught up in life's moments, trying to make a buck for his family. He was looking for extra cash flow. Now he can see what that cost him," she said gravely.

"I'm just glad he's getting out." I had my own secret reasons for wanting Colt to get out, and they were two-fold. "I appreciate you showing me around a bit more, but I do have to get back."

"I understand. Come on, let's make our way back to the house then."

I knew for certain that Bella was in good hands. I said goodbye, mentally, to the horse and gave Bella a hug. "Soon, your father will be here to give you a hug."

"I hope so. Thank you, Ms. Atwood, for checking on me. I appreciate it. I like you. You're a nice lady." Seeing a little girl happy in foster care was a social worker's dream.

"Thank you, and you are a sweet, smart little lady. See you next time."

She flapped her little hand at me as Cheryl held her hand up in goodbye. I waved to both of them and made my way to the office. Damn, I forgot the eggs. I cursed as I rode back to the office.

Even though the visit to see Colt's family gave me momentary relief, my blood pressure shot right back up as I thought about Hector. As I fumbled around in my brain for the answers, my phone rang.

"You have a collect call from USP Atwater. Do you wish to pick up the charges? Please state yes or no clearly."

"Yes," I replied.

"Hello, Amber speaking."

"Hi, Amber. It's Colt. I think I have a solution to your problem."

COLT

The promise of freedom can kill you. It can break your mental state into a thousand jagged pieces and leave you waiting for every moment to pass. All I had to do was stay out of trouble, but the ticking of time was killing me.

"Aye. What's good, farm boy?" Errol heard me thumping on the prison wall.

I was tired of being caged in. Some days were better than others. I would look at the wall and think about Bella and her big smile. Other days were not so good, and I wanted to die thinking of what happened to Anna. I'd made my bed, though, so I had to lie in it.

"Nothing. Stir crazy. I'm waiting for Frank to send word."

"Right. You think he's going to be able to find Anna's killer?"

"I do. He's the man. I have another problem now. I have to speak to Austin. He wasn't in the yard yesterday, though," I mumbled.

"Try again. Austin's always around. He ain't going nowhere, you know that. You better keep your head down. Raymond's sniffing around here like a dog in heat. You don't want any beef. He's notorious for trying to break guys before they leave. He's done it with five guys now. He managed to keep them here."

I winced when I thought about it. "I know. Don't remind me. Is he on duty today? I guess it doesn't matter if he sends his in-house goons, too," I answered my own question.

"You've never lied. He doesn't care for the law, even though he's supposed to be on the right side of it. That's why I stole."

I snickered and banged the underneath of the upper bunk where Errol was sitting. "You are full of shit, Errol! You steal because you want money and fame."

He started laughing. "You damn right."

Light footsteps padded toward the cell. Restrained tension eased from my shoulders as I looked out and saw it was a woman guard. Her hard-nosed gaze penetrated the cell.

"Y'all ready or what? Hitting the showers today, Colt?" Just like the others, she held her hand over her prized possession—the brutality baton.

"Yep. I'm ready to go."

"Errol?" she asked.

"Yes, ma'am."

"Then let's go, boys."

Same shit, different day. We made our way to the yard. There was no point in showering before then. I spotted Austin in the yard. He was sitting on the bench, the same as last time. Frank was with him again, and they were deep in discussion.

Frank's cool demeanor cracked slightly. I watched the edges of his mouth twitch as he spoke.

"Thought I might find you here." The overcast sky gave me the impression we wouldn't be in the yard long. "You got news, Frank?"

His steely eyes glanced around the yard. Austin sat

silently, observing the scene. I gave him a head nod, and he nodded back.

"Your guy is Thomas Peterson. White guy. Some little gangsta wannabe chump, a drug gopher for Las Balas. We got a location. I know where he eats, where he shits, and where his momma lives. It might take a couple of days. I'll send the word like I said."

I thought I would feel something else when he gave me the news—triumph or a sense of retribution—but that's not what I felt. I only felt a vast emptiness. Frank stretched his fingers back, giving me a look over.

"Okay. I got something else I need to be looked into. What do you know about Hector Atwood?"

"Ah. That kid. Word on the street is Las Balas got beef with him. All right kid. Nothing to say. He ain't brought trouble our way. Why?" Frank quizzed.

I lowered my tone as the clouds got a little grayer. I felt the chill on my skin and goosebumps starting to rise. "A friend of mine is his sister. He's out now. I just wanted to know if the kid is legit. He's got a hit out on him. Two hundred thousand down."

Austin popped out his bottom lip and got up from the bench. "Looks like rain. He's a good kid. I talked to him a few times. He got into a few brawls, and I told the guys to back off him."

"I got an idea to get Las Balas off his back. The kid's sister is my social worker. I owe her in a way. She's taken care of my daughter. I need to make sure everything is good."

Frank's cold eyes crinkled from a smile. "Ah. That nice piece that comes around every month to talk about prison reform. I would want to make sure about that, too." Frank slapped Austin on the arm, and they shared a laugh.

"She's really sweet. I think I can get the Russians involved." I ignored their innuendos, eyeing the sky again.

Frank squinted as the raindrops began to fall. "You mean Vlad's guys?" He spat to the side as the other pussies started heading undercover to shield themselves from a few droplets of rain.

"Yeah."

"Might work. The way I see it, you did the team a solid, so he has to meet you halfway."

"Exactly," I agreed.

The splattering of rain turned to heavier drops, and it coated the yard. Prisoners in their sandy uniforms started moving from the yard and ran to the entrance. I found the rain refreshing, and I wished it would wash all my sins away.

An announcement came, and then the bell. "All prisoners, please return to your cells. If the weather changes, we will run another half-hour later in the afternoon. All prisoners back to your cell blocks."

"Stay tuned, brother. Keep your head up. Be careful. You have minimal time to go. Raymond's been on the warpath. He sent two already on the south ward to the hole," Frank spoke out the side of his mouth as we marched back to our cell dens.

"I've been warned," I responded with a somber tone.

"See you on the next merry-go-round, brother," Austin said as his rangy frame departed down the prison hallway. If I had a magic wand to take these guys out of prison with me, I would.

Once back inside the cell, I called Vlad from a burner phone that was delivered to me inside of a library book. "Hey, brother."

"Brother. Good to hear from you. You all right in there? See Frank yet?"

"Yep. I've seen him. We've talked. Everything's good." I put my hand behind my head. "I need a favor."

Vlad, with his thick Russian accent, responded, "Anything. You know that. What do you need?"

"I need access to the Russians."

Vlad scoffed. "Okay. No problem. I'll have Mikakov call you. Have your phone ready."

"Done."

"Bye, brother."

Errol's soft snore was a noise I'd become accustomed to. It sounded similar to my horse's snore. That shit made me laugh, and not too much was comedy in this godforsaken pit. I drifted off to sleep and dreamt about Amber.

We were riding bareback on the golden curves of my Palominos deep into an emerald forest. We stopped midway and got off. She shook her champagne-colored hair at me as I chased her around. I caught her and laid her down in a bed of leaves. I stripped her down and devoured every inch of her voluptuous body.

I must have moaned in my sleep, as Errol's voice cut through my dream.

"Yo, farmboy. I don't know what you're doing down there, but I'd appreciate it if you stop it."

Disabled, I wiped the slobber from my mouth and adjusted the hard-on in my pants. The phone vibrating under my pillow dazed me. I punched underneath the top bunk in response to Errol's comment.

I picked up the phone. "Hello?"

"Colt. It's Mikakov. You need something?"

I woke up a little. "Yep. I need to organize something for when I get out."

"Go ahead. What is it, brother?"

"Can you cover a debt? A guy I have dealings with has a hit out on account of Las Balas."

I heard Mikakov crack his knuckles on the other end of the line.

"Las Balas, you say? I'm always happy to oblige. Anything

to make their life a living hell is fine by me. Say the word and what's next. We'll be in touch when you get out."

"Good." I shut down the phone. Two problems solved. Now the last one.

Amber and me.

AMBER

There were only three months left before Colt got out of prison. Every visit, I was more and more turned on by him. Every footstep on his property, my heart became more invested in Bella and his mother. Now he was firmly intertwined with my family affairs.

Today was my third visit out to Colt, minus the collect calls. It was a standard monthly arrangement for a mental health check and to confirm everything was okay on the inside. As I got ready in my bathroom, I added a lick of mascara to enhance my cinnamon-colored eyes. I didn't have to straighten my long, thick blond hair. It had its own set of waves going on. As I couldn't wear anything revealing to prison, I chose a form-fitting white bodysuit top covered with a blazer, long, tailored trousers, and heels. I added some fresh lip gloss to enhance my bow-shaped lips.

The rain was coming down like bullets in Merced, but inside my car, I felt like sunshine. I wanted to keep this secret crush deep inside. If anybody at work found out, I would be either fired or suspended. I was not willing for that to happen because of a crush. I had to keep my mouth shut. First, I had to drop by the Department of Human Services. I pulled up into the parking lot. I was not staying long. I just had a few things to take care of, and then I was off to see Colt.

Lucy greeted me on the walk in. "Oh. Aren't we looking fresh and dainty this morning." The slant in her eyes gave away her jealousy. Her jokes were becoming less and less funny.

"Morning, Lucy. How are you?"

She had a coffee cup in her hand, and her fingers were drumming on it. She smirked naughtily. "Not as good as you, apparently."

I shook my blond hair at her. "What are you talking about? Don't you have enough cases on your plate? What's happening with those two Mendez twins? Did you have to separate them?" I dropped my bags at my desk and diverted her attention back to work. The manila folder with Colt's information in it dropped to the ground.

"Ugh. That case is dragging and keeping me up at night. Their father is on drugs again, and he tried to show up to the mother's house, demanding to see them. He was out of his mind on coke."

"Sounds crazy." I was distracted and about to pick up the paperwork.

Lucy beat me to it. She bent her wide body down to pick up the folder and saw Colt's photo clipped inside. Her eyes popped open wide. "Is this the hunk you get to go see in the prison?"

She gasped, looking at me. The office was half-full and all heads rotated to me with great interest. Embarrassed, I snatched the file back from her.

"Give me that, Lucy," I hissed.

She put her hand on her hip, blocking me from sitting down. I hardened my gaze to the ground, pretending something was there.

"You didn't answer my question. Is this the guy you get to go see?"

"Yes, his name is Colt. If you don't mind, I have to go now. I have an appointment."

Lucy reeled back. "Oh. I would have several appointments if I could. You work it, girl." She opened her mouth, giving me a suggestive wink.

I composed myself and made a few calls, but my main focus was getting to the prison. I made a quick turnaround on my tasks and breezed back out of the door.

As I rode over, my phone rang. I fidgeted around and put the phone in its holder near the dash, pressing the green call button. I frowned as it was a private number.

"Um, hello. You're on speaker," I warned.

"Hey, big sis. It's your bro."

I almost swerved into another car in the next lane. I gripped the wheel hard and focused. I waved, mouthing sorry at the unsuspecting driver.

"Hector! Oh my God, why did you take so long to contact me? I've been worried sick about you. It's been a month." The words tumbled out of my mouth as I turned into the long road to the penitentiary.

"I had to adjust some things. I'm in San Francisco."

I swallowed down the bad feelings I harbored. "Are you okay? Are you staying with good people?"

His tone sounded even and calm. Like he was laying low and out of trouble. "I'm good. You don't have to worry, I'm staying lowkey. You heard from that guy inside? Anything he can do?"

"Yes. His name is Colt. He is connected. He's working on something. It might take some time but hang in there. As long as they don't know where you are, then you're good."

"I ain't got too many around me. I do want to come back. I can't hide out here forever. Plus, Las Balas runs out of San

Fran. It's not that far. So, either I'm going to be on the run 'till I come up with the money, and they still might kill me anyway, or I'm out and have to leave completely."

Fearful thoughts crept into my mind as I imagined the news report.

A young man, only twenty-five-years-old, was found dead today. Another taken by gang affiliations to the notorious Las Balas crew.

"None of that is going to happen. It's all getting smoothed out. Can you send me a number or something? How can I reach you with information?" I pushed. I parked in the USP parking lot, waiting for his answer.

"I will text it through. Delete it as soon as you get it. Don't let anybody see it."

"I won't. Promise. So glad you're safe, little bro."

"Well. For now."

"Don't say that. Stay positive."

"I'm trying. Anyway, listen, I have to go, but kiss Mom and Dad for me. I know they think I'm on some sort of retreat or whatever. But just give them a kiss for me."

"Sure, I will. I don't know when I'm seeing them next, though. Bye for now."

"Don't worry about it, then. Bye."

As I got everything together for the visit, I felt somewhat comforted that Hector was unscathed. I got out of my car and walked to the automatic double doors, making tracks to the administration window. Same drill as last time.

I flashed my Department of Human Services badge. "Hi, I'm Amber Atwood, and I'm here to see my client, Colt Winters."

The administration officer on the inside looked at the badge then back at me, matching things up.

"Okay, you can go through now, Ms. Atwood."

She opened the locked gate, and I went through to the same meeting room as usual. A guard stood watch outside the door. A camera sat in the left-hand corner, lurking over our conversation. My stomach danced with the lightness of butterflies as I entered the room. Colt's eyes held a strong element of hot, provoking intensity as I strolled in.

"Hi, Amber." He almost breathed my name. Hot damn.

"Hi, Colt. You're looking well." A blatant, ballsy lie. He was looking more than good. His steamy blue eyes had me hooked, along with his rippling forearms that I wanted around me. Faded tattoos peeked out the sleeves of his tawny-colored prison uniform, making him the ultimate bad boy.

"Thanks. I look as well as a prisoner can look. Granted, I won't be one for long. You look really nice. I like your lipstick." A wide, flirty grin followed the statement. So he did notice. It was worth the effort. I wanted him to look at me. I wanted him to notice.

"Thanks, Colt. It's a new color that I'm trying out."

He grabbed the water jug and poured me a glass of water, handing it to me. "With or without makeup, you look beautiful. I hope you don't mind me saying." His hooded eyes scanned me with appreciation.

"No. I don't. I can take a compliment," I answered flirtatiously.

"Good." He sank a little lower in his seat as I pulled out his documents. "I have some news for you. It's about Hector. I'm going to need your help, though. If he doesn't get this sorted out now, he's in trouble. I have three months to go. Otherwise, my hands are tied. If I can't get out, I won't be able to set up this prison debt overhaul. You scratch my back, and I scratch yours." Colt's creamy voice let me know he was a good negotiator. My tongue was dry, so I took a sip of water. I felt like I was between a rock and a hard place. I loved my brother more than anything.

"Colt. I personally don't see why that can't happen. The

crime you committed was, you know, not one of a killer. It's not like you're a threat to society. You're not a drug runner, either." I put on my thinking cap. "I think we can win an appeal of your parole denial due to overcrowding because you have the extenuating circumstance of threats to your safety. This combined with the fact you're not a threat to society and with the pettiness of the crime we have to have a good shot."

The sexual chemistry between us caused my voice to break into a croak. Colt wouldn't stop looking at me. A painful silence made the room's tiny noises seem loud.

"Are we going to address this?" He flicked his finger back and forth like a needle, indicating us.

"I mean, it's not a good situation. It doesn't look good." I slid a piece of my hair between my fingers, casting my eyes down. As I looked up, the intensity that Colt displayed was unmatched and being channeled toward me.

"I could care less what looks good, Amber. We look good. I want to get to know you better. I don't think I'm alone in this. Am I?"

Colts biceps flexed as he slid back up in his chair. My body was radiating heat from top to toe.

"No. You're not alone in it, but it's a delicate situation and one to be handled carefully. I don't want to lose my job," I declared.

Colt's handsome smile with those deep dimples made me smile. "It's okay. That's all I need to know for now. We can get back to the formalities if you need to."

I paused for a minute and took a sip of water. I needed it. "Bella is doing great. She wanted me to give you this." I slid over a picture of her patting Moonlight's head.

The last time I saw Bella, she gave it to me. She'd asked, "Can you please give this to Daddy, Amber? I know he will be worried about Moonlight. I want him to know his big girl is taking care of her. She's in good hands."

Colt lingered over the picture for a long time. I watched as the tears welled up in his eyes. In a very masculine way, he wiped them away as soon as they came.

"My sweet girl. Tell her to hold on. I'm going to be out of here. Can you do that for me?"

"Yes, of course I can. And you will be. I know the judge on your case. I'm going to make a call to him as soon as I leave."

Colt's face was stoic. "I know not to get my hopes up with these overcrowding parole board appeals, but thank you. If you can get me the fuck out of this piece of shit, I will be eternally grateful. Plus, I know I can help Hector. I know some people that owe me, and they will cover that debt. It's a done deal."

"Colt, are you sure? I don't want you taking money out of your pocket."

"No, it's not like that. It won't be coming out of my pocket. I have some associates. Probably the fewer questions you ask about that, the better."

I nodded, swallowing the lump in my throat. "Okay. I guess that's what I have for you today. We are making progress. Let me work on the parole board member and see if we can get a hearing date, at least."

"You really are an angel sent to me."

I knew I was blushing because I could feel it. "Thank you, Colt."

"If we didn't have that prison guard standing right there. I would kiss you."

COLT

Fresh pools of sweat soaked my bedsheets as I jostled with an imaginary attacker in my cell. I woke up in a rageful fit. The realism of the dream made me gasp for oxygen. Anna was flanked by two men either side of her, and both of them were injecting lines of heroin into her veins as she shrieked for help. I tried to run to her, but I was caught in a rope. I didn't make it in time. She frothed at the mouth and keeled over on her knees from an overdose.

I looked around me. On one side was the prison wall and on the other was the desk. The lights were out, and I could hear noises down the length of the prison halls, which was normal for USP. I got up and wiped the slick sweat off my chest. I ran the water in the washbasin and looked at myself.

"Get it together, Colt. Think of Bella," I whispered in the stark darkness.

As I paced the cell, another note mysteriously landed under the door. I picked it up. I ripped it open and turned on the lamp.

Lights out. The job is done. See you in the yard. OS.

I shook my fist violently as I touched two fingers to the

photos of Anna and Bella on the wall. I slicked my wet blond hair out of my eyes. A day of false redemption, for nothing could bring Anna back to me. Anna's killer, though, was dead. Only his mother would miss him. Frank was a man of his word.

That's how the Outlaws worked. If you're loyal to them, they'll be loyal to you. I'd earned my stripes, and now I was cashing in. At least the punk couldn't fuck up anybody else's life. I ripped the pieces from the envelope into shreds and threw it in the trash. I didn't want anything to get in the way of an early release. My bedsheets were wet, so I took them off, balled them in a corner, and slept directly on the lumpy mattress.

I woke to the sound of the clinking metal bars. My eyes shot open as Raymond ran his black baton along the length of our cell bars.

"Rise and shine, fellas. It's time for laundry and showering. Unless you bitches want to stink all day."

I felt my stomach cramping up as Errol and I rose up from our lackluster beds.

"No way," Errol answered.

Raymond, with his overgrown belly and new porn mustache, eyed me with too much interest. "You're getting out soon," he said. "Trying your hand at an appeal, huh, Colt?"

"I mean. Anything can happen. I might be here for the full three months. I'm not expecting much."

He rubbed his belly as the cell door clicked unlocked. "You shouldn't expect anything," he spat. "What's that shit balled up in the corner?"

"Just some sheets for laundry."

"You wet the bed or something?" He snickered, revealing his yellow teeth. If I had two bricks, I would smash this man's head between them. Instead, I let the blood rush through my fingers. Errol watched the conversation from a distance. I made the mistake of scoffing as he said it.

In a quick reflex reaction, Raymond snatched his black baton out of its holster and struck down between my shoulder blades with three swift brute force blows. "What'd you say?"

I bent over in the shock of the acute pain. I blew out a strained breath, staying hunched over. I thought I would take a leaf out of the play-dead handbook.

Errol spat out in anger. "Hey! Lay off him. He ain't doing nothing. That's police brutality."

Prisoners started crying out from behind their cells adjacent to mine that heard and saw him.

"Hey, I saw that! I'm going to report you to the warden."

"Kick his ass, Colt!"

"Yeah, Colt, fuck him up!"

Raymond put his lethal baton back in its holster. "I know you're not going to listen to them, are you?" he taunted, his stinking breath close to my ear. He turned to yell out to the other protesting prisoners. "Shut the hell up, you bitches, before you're next!"

He turned his back to me. He reeked of alcohol and sweat. I gravitated away from him as much as I could as he followed a pace behind us. I stood tall as I walked, trying to stretch out the pain radiating across my upper back.

Raymond laughed. "You'll be all right. Teach you to talk back. You have to learn your lesson, boy," he sneered and kept walking past the showers to the other end of the cell block.

"You all right, man?" Errol asked once the officer from hell was out of earshot.

"Yeah, I'm good. If he was on the outside, he would already be dead," I fumed.

Errol cocked his head to one side as we stripped and showered. "I don't know about that. If we wanted to get rid of the guy, that could be organized. You and I both know a few heavy hitters in here."

I let the hot water wash over my back, which was throbbing where Raymond hit me. "I can't be focused on that. I have an appeal to think about. I can't be getting into anything with him."

"I hear you. Hey, pass the soap, and don't drop it," Errol joked.

I handed him a cake of thick yellow soap. "Ha. You're not my type."

He laughed.

We toweled down and headed to the yard. I rolled my shoulders back and forth to lift the pain. The shit wasn't working. Austin recognized what it was immediately. "He get you, too?"

"Yeah, he did. What the fuck is his problem?"

Austin lit up a rare cigarette that he smoked from time to time. He offered me one. I refused. The sky was a little clearer today as I looked up and watched the wafting whites float by. It reminded me of my life and the way it had floated by here.

"The man is drunk on his own power." Austin pulled a drag of his cigarette as the smoke wisps hit the air. "He ought to be careful, though. He's got a few people riled up. There's talk of a prison hit. He might not make it through the night."

I put my large hand up to the left of my shoulder to self-soothe. It didn't work.

"You'll be all right, young man. I've had more than my fair share of blows. But he doesn't mess with an old man like me anymore. I'm not news to him. He just likes to throw his weight around when he sees an opening."

"Yeah, I noticed," I mumbled. "Want to spot me? I want to push some reps out. It looks like the weight bench is free right now."

Austin nodded. "No problem. Let me finish, and we'll get to it."

I watched the ash fall to the ground as I scanned the scene. Ten prisoners were gathered in the back corner. Nothing heavy, just the normal scene in the yard.

I dropped low and slid under the weight bar. Errol, who normally separated from me in the yard, came past mouthing something from the corner of his lips. "You need to be careful, my brother. There are a few guys in that group over there that know you're getting out. They ain't too happy. Stay alert."

He smiled at both Austin and me then walked off. Austin tapped me back down under the bar as I tried to get up.

"Don't pay them any mind. I know every one of those prisoners in the group. I've done favors for all of them. If any one of them tries it, they will have to answer to me. Now we got rep one on the same weight as last time. Let's go," Austin said firmly as he watched the group.

I got through my weight set with a sharp ache in my upper back. I'd endured a few fights in the yard in my time at USP, and I would withstand this one. I held steady and finished set one.

Austin looked down over the bar. "I heard you got your little problem sorted out." He arched one brow at me.

I exhaled out as I lifted the bar back up towards him. "Yep. Frank got it sorted."

"Good to hear. One more heave-ho to go. Let's get to it."

I pushed my muscles to the limit, and my biceps strained from the overload.

"You got it. Bring it up. Bring it up."

I gushed out a breath and lifted with the excess anger stored inside.

"That's it. I pushed you today to release that pain inside. Helps."

I pulled forward and sat up at the bench. Austin caught a glimpse at the top of my shoulders as I did. "Thanks. 'Preciate it."

"That's gonna turn up real nice in the next few days. Blue, purple, and yellow." He laughed heartily.

"Thanks, old man," I responded in a playful tone.

"Don't thank me. You got Raymond to thank for that."

"That I do."

The bell sounded, and it was time to go back in. I made it back to the cell with no trouble. As my emotions settled from the hit, I heard my phone ring. I lunged for it so quickly that Errol did a double-take.

"Easy, brother."

I ignored him and answered the phone. "Amber. What do you know?"

"Hi, Colt. I have a parole hearing date for you. If you want me to be present there with you, I can come. It's with sympathetic parole board members now. It will be good for them to see how far you've come. The date is Monday next week."

"Yes. I'm in. Can you help me prepare?"

"Yes, I can. I will bring notes to you. I'm confident you can get released. Stay strong, Colt."

"I will. I look forward to seeing you, Ms. Atwood." I rolled her name off my tongue shamelessly.

AMBER

The amount of chocolate I'd been eating couldn't have been good. I was stressed to the max about Hector, and my caseloads were rising. I still had to get a handle on the parole hearing for Colt, which on Monday. It had to go through. I had to save my baby brother, Hector. I bit my lip with anxiety as I made the umpteenth drive to work at the department.

I followed my usual routine as soon as I got to the office. I watered my baby Josie on my desk and turned my computer on. As if I didn't have enough on my plate, Lucy showed up to lean on my cubicle and irritate me. Her strong perfume made me want to sneeze.

"Hey, Lucy," I said wearily.

"Oh, that was a little lackluster. Have you been burning the candle at both ends?" she asked with narrowed eyes.

What was her problem lately? I coughed and kept going with my normal routine. I opened my second drawer and pulled out my coffee sachets. Her penetrating gaze was burning into my back. "No. I'm good. I just have an increase in my caseload. Sorry, Lucy, I can't pow-wow with you this morning. I have a lot of work to do."

"I see. It's all good. I have a few things to wrap up on cases, as well. How is the cowboy?"

I frowned at her as I rose from my desk, heading to the break room. "Cowboy? What do you mean?"

A few people were already in the break room, laughing and conversing. She ribbed me with her elbow to my extreme annoyance as I lifted my long hair out of my face.

"Oh, you know. Colt? I looked him up. He rides horses and has cowboy boots. I found a nice little pic of him on the internet. Oh, baby. Break me off a piece of that!"

I gave her a hard eye roll. "He's a client. I'm doing my job. You shouldn't be talking about clients that way, anyway. You know we are supposed to remain impartial." My skin crawled as I said it. I felt like a complete hypocrite.

"Somebody has their panties in a bunch. I'm just having some fun with you. Anywho, I have to go. Good luck with Colt."

A fake smile crossed my lips as I watched her ample physique walk away. I made my coffee and planned to plunge into my case files when I got back to my desk. My phone rang as soon as I sat down.

"Hello." I kept my voice low, though most people were talking on the phone, so it was okay.

"Hey, sister."

"Hi, Hector. I'm working on things. Colt is going to help you. I have to get him out first. Let me work on it."

"You have to. Word on the street is they know I'm in San Fran. Las Balas is looking for me. I don't know how the fuck they found out. Sis, you have to help me." He sounded frantic with worry.

"You and everybody else. You will have to do your best until I can get this appeal finalized. Can you move? How did they find out?" I asked in a shrill tone. I looked around to see if anybody heard. They hadn't.

"I think one of the guys low-key got some money for ratting me out. I don't know, but I'm on the move again. Call me when you find out. If I didn't tell you already, Amber, I love you, and thanks for everything."

I sighed deeply, the overwhelm making me feel like I was drowning in a river. "Why are you talking as if you're dying? Please stay safe and move now. Call me when you're out of San Francisco."

"Okay. Work your magic."

"Bye."

My golden hair was starting to annoy me, rubbing on my neck. That was the problem with having thick hair. I trawled through the case files and made several necessary calls. The day ran away from me. I was the last one left in the office, and I didn't realize it.

"Amber. It's time for you to go home." Donald came to my cubicle to chastise me.

"I hear you. I just have an appeal for one of my clients, and I want it to go well."

A solemn face peered back at me. "Amber, my dear, we can't save everyone. Heck, even if we could, they have to want to be saved. Remember that."

I stopped and started packing up my things. "I understand what you're saying. I guess I'm a social worker for a reason."

"That you are. You deserve as many medals as you can hold. After you finish with that appeal, I want to talk to you about a possible promotion. To oversee your division."

I did a double-take at my boss in shock. "I mean, I didn't know you were looking at me for promotion. That is...amazing!"

"Nothing is set in stone, but there's going to be some restructuring, so yes, your hard work is paying off."

I walked out to my car with a little bit of a smile on my face, deciding that was not a bad way to end the day.

The room smelled of legalities. I was in a small room where they hold parole board hearings. Bella and Cheryl were in the background. I was so glad they could make it. Colt was dressed in his prison jumpsuit that fit his muscles like a glove. He wore the jumpsuit. It didn't wear him. His square jaw was set with a serious look on his face. His closely cropped blond hair made him look like a male model. His hotness made me uncomfortable, and given the heat between us, all this hearing did was ignite a dormant flame inside my belly.

I'd managed to call in a favor from a friend, a former criminal defense lawyer, to assist with the parole board hearing appeal. Colt had everyone in his corner. His early release from jail also had a lot riding on it for me. The life and death of my little brother, Hector.

"Thanks again for coming. I appreciate it." I earnestly appreciated Bernie's involvement.

"Hey, you're welcome. I've been getting kind of bored lately. Happy to support." Bernie was an easy, laid back, retired California lawyer in his late fifties, but he was a complete shark for his clients. Every now and then, he took on a case or two, depending on whether he felt like paddleboarding instead. One of the parole board members, with his glasses hanging off the end of his nose, addressed all of us. His worn face was full of wrinkles with a droopy chin.

"We are here today for an expedited appeal concerning the case of Charlie Winters. Please state your case."

Bernie established that Colt should have been eligible for parole based on overcrowding because of his extenuating circumstances. Therefore, he should not have been denied parole before because he was a non-violent offender and did not present a threat to society. In addition to these facts there was also a threat to his safety while he remained incarcerated. As part of the proceedings the state of California allows additional statements regarding the defendant's family history and danger to society. As part of that process, I was asked to provide testimony.

"I am Amber Atwood, a social worker from the Department of Human Services in Merced and prison advocate at USP Atwater Correctional Facility. In his four and a half years served at Atwater, Charlie Winters has displayed exemplary behavior amongst his prison mates. He has been part of an in-house group program for business. We are seeking early release to care for his seven-year-old daughter, Bella, and to ensure his safety."

The board members smiled warmly at a shy Bella, who was hiding behind her grandma's leg.

"I see. What leads you to believe that Charlie's safety is at risk at this point?"

"Well, we would like to show you injuries sustained just last week from a correctional officer, Raymond Silvers."

Bernie stepped in with photographs of Colt's black and blue back. The board members looked at the photos and then back at Colt.

"Charlie, do you have anything to say to support your appeal?"

Colt stepped forward with a stern yet handsome face. "Yes. My daughter Bella is everything to me. She has suffered enough for my mistakes, which I deeply regret. I want to be there for her during this crucial time of her going to school. My mother and father are taking care of my child, but they are getting older and need to get back to their life. They have held down the fort for close to five years for me. I want to give them their life back. I want to do better. When I was first convicted, I understood I needed to own up to the conviction. Today, I stand before you a changed man. My family should no longer suffer for my mistakes. Death threats have been made against me in prison."

The parole board members turned to each other to discuss how they should move forward. I couldn't make out what they were whispering about, but I saw one of them briefly look over at Bella and smile before they faced Colt to deliver their decision.

"I do understand your circumstances. I also know that you suffered the loss of your child's mother, which no child should ever know." He looked affectionately in Bella's direction as she sank farther behind her grandmother's leg. "I hereby approve your appeal for early release. You are free to go, and I will organize for your belongings to be picked up. Congratulations on serving your time, and may you be a pillar of strength for your family. Thank you."

Cheryl's quiet tears came out as she clasped her hand over her mouth. She hugged her son's neck, and Colt's smile couldn't have gotten any brighter. Bella ran to her father's leg and hugged it tightly. He rubbed her back and lifted her up to him. She laid her head on his chest as the judge left the chambers. I smiled as I watched the scene.

This moment reinforced why I did the job I did. In less than twenty minutes, the judge had deliberated on the appeal. Colt was getting out of jail.

COLT

"Let's see here. We got a watch, a busted wallet, fifty dollars, and some change. Oh, and a pair of cowboy boots. Here's your clothing." The lady pushed all of my belongings from four and a half years ago through the slot in the window.

My mother was waiting outside to pick me up. I looked back to see if I was really free. Was it really happening? My legs took me through the front as the sliding doors opened. A feeling of euphoria ran through my veins as the light of Merced warmed my face. I saluted the sun. My mother, with her hands in the prayer position, gave me a moment to process. I let the deep breaths of freedom bury into my lungs as I strode over to greet her.

"Oh, wow. My baby is coming home. I'm so happy for you!" She wept loudly as I hugged her. Her shuddering tears brought water to my eyes, as well.

"Thank you. I am forever in your debt, Mama. You did a wonderful job. I love you forever."

She placed her hand on the side of my face, looking upon me with tenderness. "You're welcome, son. It was a pleasure.

Come on now. Let's go home and get you away from this crappy place."

"I agree. Let's blow this joint. How is Bella?"

"She's just great, she's on a playdate with her grandfather. Just so you have time to acquaint yourself."

"Great. How are the horses? How's Moonlight?"

We both jumped in the car and headed for home.

My mother glanced between me and the road. "She missed you when you were gone for the first few years. She would buck people off when they tried to ride her. Once Bella sat on her, she became a different horse. I swear your daughter is a horse whisperer. She must have gotten that from you." She laughed with genuine joy.

I smiled with my heart. It was nice to see my mother like this. "How's the old man?"

"Oh, you know, your father is as grumpy as ever. But he is excellent. If he is quiet for too long, I start to get worried." She laughed again.

I looked out the window, my eyes greedy for the undulating California hills. I touched my arms to see if they were still there. I couldn't believe I was wearing the same dirty, worn jeans and tank from over four years ago, returning to the farm.

As the driveway came into sight, I felt like a little boy again. I touched the glossy green leaves as I walked up to the porch. I let my eyes wander to the wilderness behind the property. I heard the horses neighing in the stables. I listened to the buzz of the bees in the front yard where flowers were in bloom. Home sweet home.

I walked inside, and for the most part, my home appeared untouched from the way I'd left it. I ran my thick fingers along the dining table. I picked up the picture of Anna, Bella, and me together. I had so many memories of us carved into my soul.

A sea of emotions hit me and, wanting to ground and have a moment to myself, I said, "I'm going to head down to the stables. I want to see the horses. Do you have feed down there?"

"You go on down there. Everything is in order. Your father just changed their shoes yesterday, and we got some new saddles. I think you'll like them."

Before I left, I gave my mother a kiss on the forehead. Without her, Bella would have been caught in the foster system. I owed a lot to her. I entered the barn, and Moonlight balked in her stall. She knew it was me.

"Moonlight, my beautiful mare. I'm back." The strands of her black mane shook as I picked up a nearby bucket with feed in it. I laid my hand out flat, and she nibbled on it. I stroked between her eyes. "There you go. Daddy's home. I have to take you for a ride. I heard Bella's been looking after you for a while now. Like father, like daughter, huh? You like Winters."

Moonlight snorted in derision as she licked the rest of the feed from my hand, tickling me. I walked the line and checked on my other three Palominos. I fed them, too. They were much calmer and could warm up to practically anyone. That's why I liked Moonlight. She remained icy unless you were someone she really liked. She was something special.

Speaking of special, I had important calls to make. I snuck to the back of the barn with my phone and made a call to Mikakov.

"Hey, Mikakov. I'm out."

"You're out? What, did you bust out or something? I wasn't expecting this call so soon."

"No, early release. Listen. I'm calling in that favor. Can you set a meeting with Las Balas to cover the debt? Tell them Hector is coming."

"Yes. We can set it. Let's talk later in the week. I'll come back with a date. Give you some time to acquaint yourself."

"Thanks."

I hung up quickly. The last thing I wanted was to be hanging on the phone line with a Russian. I sat right there on the haystack for a good half hour, just cherishing life. Nothing would be the same again. Anna's killer was dead, but it didn't take the burning grief from my heart. I made another call. The most important one.

"Hey."

"Hi. Welcome home," Amber said brightly.

"Thank you. I've set up the meeting to settle the score."

"Thank you, Colt."

"I want to see you. I want to take you horse riding. I can come to pick you up on the bike." I decided to be plain and upfront, with no games.

"Colt, I don't want to ruin anything for you. I don't know—"

I cut her off. "Do you feel the way I feel? I need to know. I want to be with you. Just let me show you. Let your hair down for the day." I grinned.

"Since you twisted my arm, I will. When?" she asked breathily.

"How about Friday? You can stay for dinner if you want."

"Okay. I do feel what you feel. It's a little scary, actually."

"What's scary about two people wanting to be together? I want you, and you want me."

AMBER

I'd never been in a place more peaceful than Colt's property. Baggage from cases melted right off my shoulders, floating to the ground and under the earth. I wasn't ashamed to say I took Friday off. I wanted to meld into Colt's world. The house was dead quiet when I arrived. Bella was at school and not due back until the afternoon. It was just me and the sexiest man alive—Colt Winters. Outside of the jail, he appeared larger than life—big, strong, and capable with sturdy hands and a nice pair of tanned cowboy boots. We were in his barn not long after I arrived.

Colt was coaching me onto one of the Palominos. "She won't bite. Put your foot in the stirrup, and I'll give you a leg up and over."

"Okay. Okay. I think I got it."

I held on to the bridle like Colt said, putting my right foot into the stirrup. I watched the Palomino's tail swish flies away. Colt placed his large hand near my buttocks and helped me onto the horse, leaving me feeling flushed.

"Great job. Okay, just sit tight, and I will ride beside you.

The Palominos are really gentle. Everybody rides them, and there's nothing to fear." Colt's pacifying tone, along with his cool ocean-blue eyes, made me believe every word he said. I watched the power exude from him as he mounted another one of the Palominos, his thick thighs taking up space on the horse. I eyed them hungrily.

With Colt beside me on his horse, I said, "I haven't ridden since I was a kid. The world feels different up here."

"Sure does, doesn't it? You look mighty fine on a horse, Amber. Follow me, and everything will be good. Just gently pull the reins in the direction you want the horse to go. You don't have to kick hard, just lean a little. She will know. We are just going to trot. You don't need to come up out of the saddle for that."

I nodded and followed Colt's strong lead to the letter. My hair was pinned up high and out of my face, though a few tendrils fell. My blue jeans were stretchy, so I felt comfortable on the horse. My off-the-shoulder top was keeping me cool from the muggy California heat. The clouds were a little overcast as I looked up, and a fine mist was hanging over the cobalt blue sky, threatening rain.

Colt and his trusty steed trotted alongside me like old friends. I breathed in and let all the stress roll off my back. I enjoyed the smell of the trees along the trail. The only things I could hear were blue jays and the crunching of hooves connecting with the dirt path underneath us. Riding with Colt was the first time I'd felt at ease with life. I rode in front through the overhanging branches into a wooded forest area, almost like an open enclosure. I gasped at the discovery and looked at Colt.

"This is incredible!" I couldn't close my mouth from the shock of it all. I was surrounded by a natural wonderland with all sorts of sights and sounds.

"This is my thinking space. I come here to get away from everything." Colt dismounted first and tied up his Palomino to the nearby oak tree. He placed his hand on the rear of the Palomino to let the horse know he was there as he approached.

"Hey, now. You did well. Let's get Amber off," Colt said to my horse with tenderness.

Who would have thought this big, muscled cowboy would have a hidden softer side? He stroked my horse's head. Colt touched my thigh, and I felt like sparks ran off his fingers and straight through my bloodstream.

"Here, let me help you down," Colt said as he held out his large hand to help me down from the majestic golden horse.

I jumped and slid down the horse into his strong grip. He held me there, his eyes hooded over, twirling my hair through his fingers. A powerful magnetism sank me into him further. Suddenly shy, I looked into his chest. I gently placed my hand over his chest and felt the rhythm of his heart vibrating through my fingers.

"Amber." The urgency in his voice turned me to water.

"Mmm?"

His eyes merged with mine, taking me to another galaxy as our lips merged. The weight of his passion crushed my lips. I moaned involuntarily. Colt's massive hands cupped my buttocks as he moved me away from the horse, who neighed in support.

I curled my hands into his closely cropped blond hair. The forest sounds circulated around us as my mouth was rocked by Colt's assault. He picked me up and grinned. I giggled with happiness. He pulled back from me for a beat, then turned and opened a brown satchel that was attached to the side of his horse, pulling out a flannel blanket and two plastic cups along with a bottle of white wine.

"I didn't know you had that in there! Wow. I feel special."

"That's because you are, Amber." He laid the blanket down on the forest floor, where a beam of light shone through our little forest canopy. I took it as a sign we were meant to be here. Colt noticed it too and looked up.

"Would you look at that? Four and a half years in the hole, not seeing the light like this. I'm thankful."

Colt lowered to the blanket, and so did I. He poured the white wine in my glass and then his.

"I want to propose a toast to new beginnings and starting over."

I solemnly lifted my glass. "To fresh starts."

I took a big gulp, and so did Colt. The palpable energy of raw sensuality engulfed us like a cloud until I almost couldn't breathe. Colt put his cup down, and so did I. He zoned in on my lips again and drew me to him with one hand. He ran his hand through my thick hair as we continued kissing. We ended up intertwined together, rolling on the flannel blanket. His breaths were ragged with exposed desire.

I drew back from the kiss for breath. I flicked my tongue out in concentration, deftly unbuttoning his shirt to reveal a tightly muscled chest. Colt's eyes had moved into another dimension of desire. He returned the favor, lifting my top over my head in one flowing motion. I wriggled out of my jeans next. Colt's eyes gobbled up my body. He made me feel sexy.

He groaned. "Amber, your body is a sin."

"Let me see what you're working with." My confidence was through the roof as Colt took off his pants. The large bulge told me he had more than what was required to quell my rampant desires.

"Good enough for you, queen?" he asked in an alluring tone.

"More than good enough," I muttered.

My whole body ached for Colt's touch. We didn't waste any more time talking. I felt Colt restraining himself as he trembled, running his lips down my neck. As he reached my breasts, he pulled off my bra and got to work, nibbling and kneading with precision. The sensations and the energy of the earth made me grab his head, nestling it between my breasts. He groaned.

He turned me over and continued his downward travels, kissing every place that skin showed. I was in complete surrender in the middle of his forest. He moved his hand to the top of my underwear. The wind glazed through with a few lone leaves drifting down to the ground next to me. He slipped his hand inside, finding my hot center. My walls stretched around his fingers as he entered softly, caressing me from the inside. I let out a contented, earthy sigh.

I reached down and wriggled out of my drenched underwear. Colt's firm hands all over my body had me in a hot frenzy. His head dropped between my legs, and his light stubble touched my opening, heightening all manner of sensations. The birds called out as I did. He was relentless in exploring, and I rocked from side to side, moving with him. He settled me in place by sliding both his hands under my buttocks to hit the nub of my pleasure zone.

I cried out with delight as he hit the right spot. I exploded into heavenly bliss. Colt came up for air, and I was so caught up in the earthy rapture that I didn't notice his underwear was off. His cock glistened with the shards of light hitting it. I opened to receive him. I breathed a sigh of relief as Colt lifted his weight over me, moving, gliding, possessing me into submission.

I watched the exquisite agony as he tried to control himself from plunging into the depths of pleasure. I grabbed his back in a primal move, anticipating his fall over the edge. He almost looked to be howling to the moon as the orgasm claimed him. More leaves dropped to the ground as we lay there in our nakedness in the forest. The horses neighed. They knew something magical had just happened.

I giggled. "Think they were watching us?"

Colt wrapped the edge of the blanket over me as he rolled to face me. He smirked. "Probably getting tips."

"Wow. Just wow."

"I have been cooped up a while. Sorry if I hurt you."

"No, you didn't. I enjoyed every minute of it, cowboy."

Colt stroked my belly, eyeing my breasts hungrily. "I want to let you know I'm setting up the meeting for your brother tomorrow, so he's going to need to come back to town. I will keep him under my wing."

"You will?" I confirmed.

Colt smiled and twirled my hair in fascination. "Of course. I never break a promise."

I breathed out all my troubles. Just for the moment.

"Don't worry, I will protect you and yours like you have done for me, Amber. You're important to me," Colt reiterated.

"Thank you." The wind picked up a little, and goosebumps raised on my arms.

"I want to lay here with you until the end of time, but I have to get back. Bella will be back, and this will be the first time I've seen her outside of the prison."

I slowly picked up my clothes and put them back on. Colt did the same.

"I understand. I don't want to intrude, so I will leave you with your family."

Colt lightly touched my fingers, picking them up and kissing them. "You are part of it if you want to be. You're welcome to stay. Please stay for dinner." His blue eyes held nothing but the truth.

I touched his cheek. "I would love to."

We mounted the horses and made our way back. The whole way back, I could feel my center and all the places Colt had possessed, and it felt damn good. I would never forget this glorious day.

COLT

"Mikakov. What's the word?"

"Set in three days. Warehouse off East Mission Avenue. Eight o'clock. Las Balas thinks Hector is going to be there, but they are set to get a rude awakening. We got you covered. We figured on the account you didn't turn into a snitch bitch, we will take the debt. Morcov will shoot the whole Las Balas crew if they try anything."

"Thanks, Mikakov. I'll be there."

"Keep connected. We will give you instructions closer to the day, brother. You served your time, and for that, you won't be forgotten."

"That's the Outlaw code."

"Indeed. Take care 'till then."

I had a few stops to make. I stepped out from the barn and into the heat. Right now, it was the only place I could really have a conversation. I didn't want Bella to even suspect anything. My mother had gone back to her house, and it felt weird not to have her here. Amber was a guiding light in not only my life but Bella's, too. I couldn't wait to be with her again. Every part of my hot-blooded manhood wanted to claim her body again.

I checked the horse's feed and cleaned up a little in the barn. Pigeons flew in and out, cooing. They'd made a nest, it seemed, at the top of the barn. I watched as they strutted back and forth across the top row beams.

"What do you think about them, Moonlight? You made some new friends." Moonlight seemed to comprehend my ramblings to her. She reared her head at me, wide-eyed in response. "All right, they can stay."

My phone was running red hot. This time, I saw it was Diego, founder of the Merced Outlaw chapter. I had been avoiding the call for a minute. I wasn't sure when I would resume, or if I would.

"Hey, Diego. What's new, brother?"

"You tell me. You haven't called to check in. I wondered how you were since you got out. Frank told us he spent some time with you on the inside."

I winced as I neared the house. "He did. Truth be told, I have some things to handle. I'm not in a rush to come back. If I do, I can't be doing deliveries. It's not a good look for you or for me. I'm on parole, so I can't fuck up," I whispered with a punch.

"I hear you. We don't want to put you in a compromising position. You served your time. I have a legit side hustle for you at the motorcycle repair shop if you want it. No hot parts. I promise. Think it over. I know you got the farm and stuff, but I wanted to extend the offer."

"Thanks, Diego. I appreciate that. How is Misty doing? Has she given birth yet?"

"She is ready to pop. I'm glad because she is extra loco, more than normal."

I laughed and felt sorrow hit my heart as I thought of Anna pushing Bella into the world. Now she wasn't here to see her grow. The revenge inflicted on her behalf was bittersweet for me. "I know that feeling. I will think about things and get back to you."

"Good. Take care, and if you need anything, just pick up the phone."

"I will."

I was at the front door. I pulled off my cowboy boots and entered. Bella was at the kitchen table, drawing what looked to be a horse in crayon. I kissed the top of her head and sat down with her. The next part of the conversation I knew was going to be hard. I played with one of the crayons, scanning her happy face. I didn't want to make her sad.

"Whatcha drawing, baby girl?"

Bella, with her innocent spirit, looked at me with the eyes of her mother. "It's a horse, Daddy."

Bella's hair was in a ponytail because that's all I knew how to do. My mother was a little better than me, but Bella liked it.

"I love it. You're doing a really good job." She swung her feet under the table and licked her little pink tongue out as she drew the outline of a tree for the horse. "I have something to ask you, and you can say no if you want to."

She looked up at me with eagerness. "I'm nearly finished. You can ask me. What is it, Daddy?"

"I wanted to ask you if you want to go see Mommy?" I pushed down the lump of coal lodged in my throat.

Bella grew silent, and I instantly regretted making her leave her happy place. She put her ponytail into her mouth nervously. "I want to see Mommy. But how can we? She's in the ground. We can't see her. She speaks to me sometimes, though. She tells me to put my shoes away."

I reached out and took her soft little hands in mine. The tears formed water wells, and I couldn't help but let one fall. I wiped it away quickly.

Bella looked at me with curiosity, placing her little palm on my stubbly chin. "Daddy, don't cry. Mommy is in a better place. I think she's having fun. Granny told me that. I want to see her, so we can go, but don't cry, Daddy."

Such a sweet child. She went back to swinging her legs and singing a little song to herself.

"Okay. Will you be free from drawing in an hour? How about we eat something first?"

"Yay!" She raised her arms in the air and ran around the table. This was a Bella I would need to get to know. I didn't even know my own daughter. She had turned into this emotionally intelligent, bright, energetic soul that soothed me. She was the one being strong and not me.

This whole cooking thing was new to me, too. Anna used to cook, but I had to try for Bella. I'd learned a few recipes in prison, so I felt like I could do the basics.

"How about some grilled ham and cheese? Sound good?"

Bella nodded her head. "I'll get the ham and cheese. I cook with Granny sometimes. She taught me." She opened the refrigerator and put the ham and cheese on the counter. I was in awe of her.

"There you go, Daddy. I'm a big girl now," she said defiantly.

I bent down to her height. "You don't always have to be a big girl. I'm home now. Daddy will take care of you, okay?" I lightly tapped her cute little nose.

"Okay. I like to help. It's fun to cook."

I smirked. Maybe in the future, when she had to cook all the time, she might not think it's so fun. For now, I indulged her. I rustled up some ham and cheese sandwiches and put them in the waffle maker. We ate in silence, and then I put Bella's jacket on to go. As soon as it was on, she ran out the front door.

"Bella! Where are you going?"

"I'm going to pick some flowers for Mommy. She likes flowers. She planted some at the front."

Again, I had to wipe the water from my face. Bella picked a few red geraniums from the front, along with some purple bluebells. I knew Anna loved bluebells. I gave her the time to gather them. She ended with a small bunch, which she thrust proudly at me.

"Here we go. She will like these."

I hugged my daughter to my leg. "Yes, baby girl, she will. Let's go."

We took the car. I was not ready to take Bella on the bike just yet. I wanted her to be a little older before I did that. I drove through the Merced backstreets to the cemetery. As soon as we arrived in the parking lot, an overwhelming sadness washed over me. Anna was a good mother. She loved Bella more than life itself. I struggled to stop the tears from falling. I wanted to be strong for Bella.

"Daddy, I think maybe it's okay to cry. Ms. Atwood said it was okay. I just don't want to see you sad." Her little hand's warmth landed on top of mine, and I held it.

"Thank you, sweetie. Your mother would be proud of the young lady you've become."

She hugged me, and I vowed to protect her with every cell in my body. I gathered myself and got out of the car. She walked with me, and it took us about twenty minutes to find Anna's gravestone from where my mother said it was.

A gray, rounded tombstone was right in front of me with Anna's name carved in it. Bella placed the flowers in front of it, patting the soil. I ran my fingers over the engraved letters. I had some things I wanted to say.

"Anna, I'm sorry I couldn't be there for you in your darkest hour. Please forgive me. I just want you to know it's been handled." My voice choked up as I struggled to release years of pent-up grief from my system. "I want you to know that I loved you so much. I wanted to marry you. I'm sorry for everything. I hope you're resting easy up there."

I pointed to the sky, and Bella pointed with me.

"Mommy, we love you. I know you forgive Daddy. I hope you like the flowers."

My heart swelled with pride at the maturity of my little daughter. I felt the guilt creeping up in me. I didn't want more put on Bella than she could handle. I let the wind of death cross over us as we said our goodbyes to Anna.

We left, hand in hand, a little lighter for it.

AMBER

"You need to come back. It's being organized. Two days to go. Can you make it undetected?" I asked my brother Hector. I paced in the breakroom in nervousness. Lucy sauntered in, and instantly, her eyes reached me.

"I can. I will hit the road today," Hector replied.

I kept circling the breakroom. "Where are you staying when you get back? Do they know about me?"

I swiftly looked around and caught Lucy's eye. She was still watching me. I winced. She was the last person I wanted to see right now. She threw me a wave with her fingers. I rolled my eyes to myself and kept pacing.

"Stop stressing. Colt called me directly. We are handling it. We don't want you involved. I will be back, and no, I'm not staying with you if that's what you're worried about. I'm going to roll with Colt till the deal is done."

I huffed and puffed a little. "I'm worried about you, that's all. If Colt has it under control, then I trust him."

"Ah. It sounds like you and Colt have something going. You getting it on with the cowboy, sister?" Hector's tone changed.

The rush of red was making my cheeks flushed. I stopped in place. Lucy's eyes were observing my every movement. She was becoming annoying these days. I could only handle her in small doses. I turned my back to her.

I ground my teeth a little. "I'm not talking to you about this right now."

"Okay. Just know everything is okay. I will see you soon."

"All right, bye." I tried my hardest to ignore Lucy and talk to some of my other colleagues. She tugged at my shirt as I tried to walk past.

"Hey, how are you doing? Did I hear you mention that cute cowboy's name right then?"

I gave her a cold stare in an attempt to move her on. "No, you're hearing things, honey. I was talking to my brother. I have a pretty heavy workload, so I will have to catch up with you a little later."

Lucy narrowed her beady eyes at me as she sipped her drink. "Right," she concluded.

I made my way back to my desk. I texted Colt because I was so nervous about everything.

Please take care of my brother.

He texted back seconds later.

Nothing will happen to him.

Tameka, a long-standing staff member in the department and one of the most dedicated social workers on my district team, came to my desk. "Hi, Amber."

I broke into a smile. It was hard not to smile at Tameka. She was standing at the edge of my cubicle with a frown.

"How are you?"

"I'm doing great. I just wanted to say congratulations to you."

Puzzled, I looked back at her weirdly. "Congratulations? What do you mean?"

"What, you don't know?" She pointed to the door of my boss's office.

"What am I supposed to know?" I asked slowly. Now I felt anxiety knocking at my door, setting to make my day just a little more on edge.

She gave the face of a naughty kid who did something they shouldn't have. "Oh. I made a boo-boo. I don't want to ruin it. Me and my big mouth."

"Now you and your big mouth need to tell me what's going on."

She paused and read my face. "I think you might have a promotion. Bossman is singing your praises right now."

My boss rounded the corner just as Tameka finished speaking. He gave a solitary wave, beckoning me in his direction. I quickly stepped into his office, sensing Lucy's antenna go up as I did, and shut the door behind me.

"Hi. How are you doing?"

"I'm doing really well," I lied. I wanted Hector home, and I had been stressed out ever since Colt told me what was about to go down.

"Please, take a seat."

I assessed my boss. He was a calm and centered man. He stood on the side of justice, and if cases involved children, he bent the rules to make sure they were taken care of. "I want to officially welcome you to the management team. We have been reviewing all your case files for the last year. Your record is impeccable, and you have made solid decisions in challenging circumstances. I especially like the work you're doing with prison reform. I see that you were able to get your last client home to his daughter early. How is she settling in now that her father's back?"

"Pretty good, so far. Colt is adjusting back to life on the farm and running the business. Cheryl still comes and goes so she can help him with Bella. He is doing well overall."

He nodded. "Great. We want you to step into the role next month. So you have about three weeks to hand over."

"Can I ask why the position wasn't advertised? Aren't some people going to be mad about that?" I asked.

"No. I make the decisions at this branch, and you are heads above the rest of the team. That's not taking away from them at all. Just how it is. Please don't tell them I said that."

I found that to be a little harsh, but I kept my thoughts to myself.

"Will you accept?" he asked.

"Yes. I would love to oversee the team. I know them well, and everyone is solid."

"Good. I'm going to lower your caseload and give you more managerial responsibility. I will have Sonya work with you to oversee and train you. You will find an extra ten thousand a year in your salary, along with bonuses."

"Wow. Thanks for believing in me."

"Always have. Now go out and save more lives. Thanks, Amber. HR will send the contracts through to you via email."

I was stunned. All areas of my life were elevating at a rapid rate. "Thank you!" I beamed at my boss and left the room.

All I thought about was the first person I wanted to share the news with—Colt. I ran out of the department to sit on the back step and called Colt's phone.

"Hey!"

His husky laughter made me swoon. "Hey, pretty lady. Are we still on for tonight at my place?"

"Yes, we are. I wanted to share something with you."

"Please." He waited patiently.

"I just got a promotion! I can't believe it."

"Baby, I'm so happy for you. We can have a celebration tonight. Glad you told me now. And the great thing is your brother will be riding in."

My mood dropped as soon as he said something about Hector. "Do you think they will find him? I'm not sure about things, Colt."

"Let me paint this scenario for you. If they show up, I will call a whole gang of not only Russians but Outlaws, and they will be executed at first sight. A Las Balas crew member wouldn't dare show up on an Outlaw Souls property unless they want bloodshed."

"I trust you, Colt."

"Do you? Because you seem shaky. I made a promise, and when I make one, I keep it," Colt responded with conviction.

"I believe you. I can't wait to see you and Bella tonight. I just have to keep things a little quiet here. I never really thought about us and how it would impact...you know, if anyone found out."

"Baby. None of that shit is going to matter when you and I get married."

I held the phone away from my face in shock. "Colt! We barely know one another. You are one crazy cowboy," I proclaimed.

"No. I'm not. When you're in jail with your life in your hands every single fucking day, you have time to contemplate what's real in life. I know what I want. I lost Anna. I'm sure as hell not going to lose you, too. I didn't say right now. I just feel what I feel, so I'm saying it," Colt said vehemently. His strong-willed voice and resilience turned me on. A leak was springing between my legs. I breathed out slowly.

"Colt, you are..."

"I'm what? Talk to me, Amber. I need this."

A presence floated around the back of me, and I angled to the left to see who it was. None other than Lucy with a smile that didn't reach her eyes. I shut down the phone like lightning, hanging up on Colt. I wondered how much she heard. I held my stomach in.

"So, I guess congratulations are in order." The dry sarcasm in her tone was hard to miss.

"Not if it's not genuine," I fought back.

"Why wouldn't it be genuine? I just want to say there is a huge breach of conflict of interest if you're involved with a client. But you know that, right? Since you're going to be my boss and all."

She sucked in a breath through her teeth, and an evil smile came out.

"I don't know why on earth you would be telling me that. I know the rules." I felt the sweat trickling down my leg and into my shoes.

She gave a half-baked laugh, sauntering back to her desk.

COLT

I kept the guns away from the house. I didn't want Bella's eyes to ever come in contact with that part of my life. Not even my mother knew where the guns were stored. I climbed up to the attic of the barn. Underneath a heavy stack of hay, a large artillery box was housed. Enough bullets were in it to take out a whole army. I had a solid selection of military hand grenades and two semi-automatic pistols. I also had a long-range sniper rifle and a taser for good measure. I zeroed in and checked their chambers. They were loaded with bullets and ready to go. My secret weapons.

Amber's voice rang loudly in my head. "What if they come to your house? What will you do?"

Time to lock in. No part of me waned in confidence. When you have the Russian mafia backing you, much is possible. These motherfuckers would blow your head off and return to eating breakfast like nothing happened. I knew because I'd seen it already. I flashed back to the vivid memory of that morning.

"So you want to play, you piece of shit?" Mikakov delivered a

bone-crunching body blow to the dealer who dared cross him by not paying him for a drug trade.

An unwise street dealer was tied up with blood oozing from his swollen left eye. As he talked, blood bubbled up to his lips and stained his teeth. He spat it out. Both of his hands were tied behind him with rope. "I told you, motherfucker, I don't know who has your money. If I did, I wouldn't tell you, either. Eat shit and die."

Bad move. Mikakov didn't take too kindly to him saying that. He clenched his fists in his black leather gloves and simply said, "Okay. I'm going to give you another shot because I'm a nice guy."

A large, wrinkly, bald-headed guy aimed his pistol straight at the dealer's temple and fired. The bullet went clean through the center, right between the eyes.

Mikakov moved closer to the limp body and said, "No, motherfucker, you eat shit and die." He looked to his crew, summoning them. They laughed, leaving the abandoned warehouse. "C'mon, let's go eat breakfast."

The sound of the pigeons cooing in the barn loft brought me back to the moment. Timely, as that's when my phone rang.

"Hello?" The call was coming from a private number.

"Hi, Colt. It's Hector. Close call."

"How so? You're nearly here, right? Your sister is going to be here for dinner tonight."

"I'm on my way. Ran into an issue. Las Balas somehow found me in San Fran. I had to move locations. I moved to the second location, and somebody tipped them off. I got a call that they came looking at the second spot an hour after I left." Hector's voice was shaky with fear.

"Stay calm. You're on the road, right?"

"Yeah. I'm about an hour away."

"How do you think they're tracking you?"

"I don't know. I wasn't running in the same circles since I got out. Maybe they followed me." Hector's shaky voice let me know that danger could present itself. I peered down at my artillery. I had enough if something popped off. Bella's girly laughter rang in my ears. I closed my eyes.

"Are you strapped?" I asked.

"Yes. I got a Glock. I'm good. I don't want to bring trouble to your family, man. Maybe I should just keep riding, you know?"

"No. You're not. We are going to face what's coming. All the players are in place. You can't back down now. We are going in headfirst. The Russians are on our side, so there's no reason to be fearful. You will be safe here. They ain't coming here to the farm."

"See you soon."

"Peace, brother. Ride safe."

I closed the box but grabbed the semi-automatic. I tucked it in the back of my waistband, which I'd strapped up with a holster this morning.

I climbed down from the barn loft, walking with a purposeful stride to the house. I got another phone call when I got to the barn door and stopped. I read the screen —Amber.

"You hung up on me, baby," I said.

"Sorry. I had to. A nosy work colleague was standing behind me, and I think she knows about us. I'm freaking out a little bit. If she reports me, it could turn into a whole investigation. I could lose my job, and they might send you back." Amber's sweet voice rushed through the phone with all kinds of scenarios.

"Baby. Does she have any proof of anything? Remember, you're part of my parole. I have to see you by law to check up on my daughter. Even if you were talking to me on the phone, she can't prove that you and I are together."

A rush of air was expelled through the phone. "You're right. That makes sense. See you tonight."

"See you tonight. I'll help you clear your head." I let those words roll off the tongue silkily.

She giggled a little. "I'm sure you will find a way, Colt."

We hung up, and as I stood at the barn door, I eyed Moonlight.

"Are you ready for me now? Is it time for us?"

Moonlight neighed, her silky black coat shining in the Merced sun. Her head bobbed a few times in response. The equine beauty needed a rider, and that was me. On impulse, I walked to her stall door and stepped inside with the mighty horse. She backed away slightly. I breathed deeply—the dance between horse and man. I reached for her reins hanging on the left side. At this point, anything could happen. She could rear up and stomp on me. She could bite me, or she could surrender.

"Easy, Moonlight. It's just you and me. I know you like you know me. We are wild, unkempt. Forces of nature." As I moved in a stalking motion around Moonlight's side, she shuffled her hooves away from me.

I heard a little voice behind me. "You just have to touch her star, and she will stay still, Daddy."

"Bella, move back and don't make sudden movements." With no fear, Bella walked in between Moonlight and me. Moonlight bowed her head instantly, nuzzling Bella's shoulder. Bella hugged her and rubbed the middle of her forehead.

I rubbed my eyes. Bella, the horse whisperer. "You know what I want to be when I grow up, Daddy?"

"What's that, Bella?" While Bella had Moonlight in a vulnerable position, I put her saddle and her reins on.

"I want to ride and look after horses."

I strapped Moonlight up and walked around the back of her hindquarters, feeling along as I went. The last thing I wanted was to get kicked in the teeth.

"You certainly have a way with her. Where did you learn that?"

Bella shrugged, her little pigtails shining in the daylight. "I don't know. I just talk to Moonlight, and she listens. Don't you, Moonlight? I love you. You're such a good horse."

"Yeah, think she'll let me ride for a minute, just to keep her in shape?"

"Yes. She likes you. She was mad because you left her for a while."

I scoffed. "Is that you or the horse talking, Bella?" I looked at the little brown eyes staring back at me.

"No. I wasn't mad. I was sad. That's all."

Moonlight raised her head, and I walked her out of the barn.

"I'm sorry, Bella. Please forgive me. I made a mistake. Here, take the reins. I trust you with her. Got to get used to her sometime, if you want to train and work with horses."

"Yay! It's okay, Daddy. I know you didn't mean it."

I stroked the top of Bella's head as I watched in complete astonishment. This little pint-sized kid had tamed the untamable horse. Moonlight trotted right alongside Bella and followed her every command.

"Un-fucking-believable."

AMBER

The water hit my face as I washed the grit and grime of the day down the drain. Another day of saving children from abandonment, assigning court dates, mental health check-ups for clients, and a plaguing concern for my brother. I toweled off as I thought about the men I was going to see. Colt with his cowboy swagger and huge, loyal heart and my little brother, a little lost but with good intent. I loved them both.

I slipped into an emerald green babydoll dress with leggings, something cute and girly, and put on some cute little boots. Colt inspired that. I pulled up into the driveway an hour later. Colt's house looked so cozy and inviting. I felt as if I was walking into another part of the earth, not the dry, often dusty California hills of Merced. As soon as it came into my sight, I slipped into relaxation. Something truly sacred and captivating existed at this property. Maybe because of its carved-out trails that led into the back of the mountains or because of all the beautiful sounds of nature that existed. The sound of the brook was something I wouldn't mind hearing every day.

My brother was standing on the front porch, puffing on a

cigarette. I had to fumble around twice to get my car door open. It was hard to contain my excitement. I ran to him, nearly knocking him off his feet. He hugged me back, a little in shock from the barrage.

"You made it! Oh my God, you made it. I was so worried." I touched his face and reared back to take a closer look at him. He held his cigarette to the side and blew out the smoke.

"I told you that I would be okay. I owe you. Both you and Colt. He's a hell of a guy."

"Yes, he is. He's a very loyal and protective man."

Colt stood on the porch with a look of amusement on his fine, chiseled face. "Am I?" Colt's mouth cocked into a quiet smile as he snuck up from behind.

"That you are," I confirmed.

"Only to the people who are loyal to me," he clarified with a steely look in his blue eyes.

Hector regarded the conversation and continued puffing on his cigarette. Colt walked past my brother and kissed me solemnly on the mouth, stealing the breath right out of me. My brother cleared his throat conspicuously.

"I see what it is now. You two." He grinned. "I'm glad you're good together. Look after my sister, Colt."

"That's the only thing I plan to do," he responded with an affectionate smile.

Colt put his arm around me, kissing my cheek. All of this affection in front of my brother made me a little shy. Colt seemed oblivious to my discomfort.

"When you find a good thing, Hector, don't let it go." Colt turned to me. "You look like heaven, baby."

Even though it was kind of embarrassing, Colt made me feel loved and seen. Despite his harrowing past and the crazy set of circumstances that had brought us together, I loved this man. I just didn't know quite how to say it.

Hector sucked in more nicotine and exhaled upward. "I'm too busy trying to stay alive to worry about women."

I squeezed his arm. "You'll find somebody for you, but I get that you need to stay out of harm's way."

Hector had let his hair grow out a little. He had a two o'clock shadow that made him appear more manly. I don't know what happened in San Francisco, but something about his demeanor had changed. My little brother was growing up fast.

"Meh." He shrugged his shoulders as we all floated inside.

Cheryl was at the kitchen counter, and the room smelled like spices and meat. I breathed in the heavenly aroma.

"Cheryl, is that casserole?"

"Yes, it is. Got a few more minutes to go, and then I will dish it up."

I observed as she wiped her brow and stood back from the oven. "Do you want some help?"

She shooed me back into the living room. "No, go sit down. No help needed."

Hector walked around, studying the pictures on the shelves as I plopped down on the couch. He picked up one of Colt on a horse with a lasso. "You really were a cowboy. This is insane. When did you do this?"

Colt replied, "I used to go to the rodeo every year to compete. I used to do barrel races as well. We had a bigger farm when I was little, more like a ranch, wasn't it, Mom?"

She licked her fingers from the casserole dish. "Uh-huh. I loved that place. So many trails. Those were the good old days. All those fresh pine trees. You used to be outside for hours, playing with that lasso. I had a hard time calling you in at night. You were obsessed."

Colt's vibrant blue eyes sparkled at his mother's recollection. "I know. I was a real scruff, too. Used to drag mud and dirt into the house."

Colt talking about his family made me think of mine. Not like I got to see my parents much since they lived in Florida. I remembered what they'd said when I first came to Merced.

"Why do you need to go all the way over there? You can just stay here in Florida. Nothing wrong with this place. California ain't got nothing on Florida if you ask me," my mother had said. With her golden hair and tanned skin from the Florida sun, she thought it was the best place on earth. My father would follow whatever my mother said. He was a yes-man. Safe to say, my mother wore the pants.

"Mama. I want to see the other side of the country. I never thought I would get the job. I want to go see it. If I don't like it, I can always come back."

I felt myself smile. That had been over six years ago. I had well and truly made a life here in Merced and would never look back.

Cheryl grabbed her potholder and got ready to take the casserole out. She continued talking about her son. "Bella is the spitting image of Colt on a horse. She's got her daddy's genes."

"I don't know what to do on a horse, but I sure know what to do on a bike." Hector laughed as he set the picture down.

"Similar in a lot of ways. You treat her right, and she will do the same. Have to talk to them nicely," Colt explained as he looked at me.

"Where is Bella?" I asked, looking around.

"Oh, she is out in the barn with my husband, Clive, who you haven't met yet."

"A real family affair," Hector observed.

"Sure is." Colt had snuggled in beside me on the couch and laced his fingers together with mine. He curved into me and spoke delicately into my ear. "Hector and I have some dealings to take care of, so we will be in the barn after dinner. Don't be alarmed."

I rotated my head in his direction. "I realize I have to trust you. I know nothing about settling scores. I want you to be careful and to know you are still on parole."

His pensive face let me know he was heeding my warning. "I understand. I won't do anything to put you or your brother in harm's way." He grabbed my hand and kissed it.

The sound of voices made me look up from our secret conversation. Bella came in, holding hands with an older gentleman. His face had been weathered by time, but he was the spitting image of Colt, only decades older. If this was any indication, Colt was going to age very well. The resemblance was so uncanny that it shook me a little. My eyes blinked to look at him again. He had the same build as Colt and wore black leather boots. His head was bald, and he was a little smaller in height. Colt must have gotten that from his mother. Clive was not hunched over and weakly by any means.

"Hello, everyone." He scanned the room and took everyone in. He turned his focus to his son.

Colt unhooked from me and stood. The respect for his father was clear as soon as he set foot into the room. He met his father halfway, and they embraced for a long moment.

"I knew you would make it home safely. Sorry I didn't get here sooner to see you," Colt's father said in a raspy voice.

"It's okay, Pop. You're here now."

It almost brought a tear to my eye to see the exchange between father and son.

"Your horses are in good shape. I might have to jump back in the saddle, my boy." He patted his son on the back, laughing with a toothy grin.

Cheryl gave him a funny look. "Last time you got on one of those Palomino horses, you fell off, remember? I had to nurse you back to health for days. You whined so much," Cheryl said.

Colt's father pursed his wrinkled lips together and moved to sit at the kitchen table. "Oh, hush, woman. Now introduce me to your friends, Colt." He smiled at us both.

Bella had her hair down and was wearing jeans, a cute little top, and, to my delight, her very own cowboy boots. She ran over to sit by me.

"Dad, this is my girlfriend, Amber, and her brother, Hector, who is staying here for a night or two." The announcement shocked me. I was as stunned as everyone else in the room. You could hear a pin drop as everyone stared at Colt and then back at me.

"Daddy's got a girlfriend!" Bella, with her big grin, was the one to break them out of their astonished silence. She covered her mouth, swinging her legs on the couch. She started giggling up a storm. She let the announcement fade and move right into the next thing on her mind. She got up after that and ran to her room, yelling, "Grandpa, I want to show you my horses! I'll be back with the drawing."

My mind spun in confusion. That reaction could have gone either way. Her mother hadn't been dead that long. She might have been angry about it. I brushed my hair out of my face.

The room was like a slow-motion movie returning to full speed. Colt stared at me, and I tried hopelessly to avoid his gaze.

"That's good, son. Just don't go back to jail," Clive warned. I saw the tension on Colt's face as he balled his fists.

Hector sat silently. I got the feeling from his blank stare that he had other things on his mind than whether Colt and I were having a love affair.

Cheryl was in disbelief. "I should have known. I mean, you spent a lot of time together."

Piping hot plates of a mixed smell of beef, sweet cinnamon, and earthy potatoes filled the air.

I walked out to the back porch. I felt embarrassed and rejected a little by Cheryl, and his father didn't exactly endorse us either. Dusk was on the menu, as well, as the sky gave us a feast of deep oranges and pale pinks mixed with royal blue in the sky. The chill made me wrap my arms around myself. A minute or two later, Colt came out. I just needed to have the cool air injected into my lungs.

A large warm arm reached around my shoulders. "Babe. I'm sorry. It just came out. I don't know why."

I turned. "Colt, I said we should be careful. I mean, we don't know what this is. You told your mother? I mean, what do I look like right now? A social worker who seduces my clients? I could get fired. I keep telling you that! You're not listening."

His pale blue eyes gazed high into the mountain tops that sat in the distance behind the property. Crickets were sounding off. This was their time. Frogs were making themselves known, as well. I listened to the sounds of nature to calm myself down.

"Might have been a Freudian slip, but I meant every word I said. My mother will get over it. It's my life. Bella loves you. I love you, Amber. That's the bottom line. I don't give a damn about anything other than that at the end of the day. My mom isn't going to rat you out. She would never do that." His blue eyes came back from their journey over the mountain tops and reached into my soul.

"I didn't know you felt that way."

"Now you know. You don't have to say it back. Prison has done something to me." He kissed my cheek, and his lips were cool from the night air. "Come on in. Time to fill your belly."

I saw the hint of sadness in his eyes, but he covered it well.

COLT

When the day of redemption comes, you pray. You drop to your knees and pray for everything good in this world. Today was the day. The operation started at the crack of dawn before the sun broke over the back of the California mountains. I stood with my cup of Joe on the porch as a pocket of orange filled the sky, and the dewdrops hit the tips of the sweet-smelling blades of grass.

I practically gulped my coffee down, then I called Mikakov.

"Morning."

"Morning, champ." Mikakov's thick Russian accent made a wry smile lift over my face.

"Confirming."

"Okay. Here's how we run. You're out of this. Know this—they are coming for blood. These bitches think Hector is going to be there. Me, Vlad, Moracov, and Pedro are going to go in. We are going to settle the price on the young man's head, on the proviso that you take him under your wing. He's yours now. Understand? But we got you covered."

"I understand. Thank you."

"No. Colt, thank you. We know the price you paid. You put your life on the line. We respect that."

I watched as a bird flew to the closest tree and called out. "See you tonight."

"Colt, keep Hector away from the scene, just in case. Sit high on the hill if you are going to be there."

"Done, and no problem taking the kid under my wing. It's what I planned to do all along."

"Good."

"Bye."

So it was done. Hector joined me outside.

"Hey, Colt. I wanted to ask you something." He had a cup of coffee in his hand and stood on the porch beside me.

"Shoot."

"Do you think I could work with you? I could use a job. I want to stay out of trouble." Hector posed his question without reservations.

"We all find ourselves in positions in life we shouldn't be in. I know that for certain. Give me some time to work on things."

"Okay. For now, let's see this thing through. I'm going in tonight," he said. "I want to be there."

"The Russians don't want you there. They're trying to save your ass. It's a bad idea."

"I know it is, but I can't just let you go into that situation, knowing that I was the cause of it in the first place."

"Yes, you can. I'm seasoned. If, for any reason, one Las Balas member sees you, they might not get you right away, but they will get you. Trust me."

"I get it. I don't want to be walking around watching my back through Merced."

I looked out as the sun broke over the hill. My little

sleepyhead Bella would be up soon. "You won't. Once the Russians stand in for you, not one person will harm a hair on your head."

"Thanks, Colt."

"You're family now, and that's what we do."

I left Hector standing outside and went to Bella's bedroom to see her face and hear her little snores as she snuggled deeper into the covers. She had pretty hair, like her mother, a face like a little angel, and a heart as big as a lion, my little girl. I wanted a better future for her.

Hector was still sitting on the front porch, and the frown on his face told me he had a lot on his mind.

"Hey, Hector, let me take you down to where the guys work. It's not crop season right now, but let me show you how it works."

I hadn't stepped foot in the farming side of the business since I'd been back. Mom had handled that side of things, so I would be seeing it for the first time along with Hector. We walked to the production warehouse as the sun's heat started to warm us up.

"What are you going to do? Are you gonna go back to working at the chop shop? I heard that's what you were into," Hector asked as we walked.

I flashed back to being hauled off in handcuffs. "No. They want me to, but in a different way. I'm an Outlaw 'till I die. I just can't do that right now. Diego runs a legit motorcycle chapter here. He made an offer. I know the cops are going to be on my ass if I do, though."

"Yeah, but if you can make money at it, why not?"

I glowered at Hector. "Have you learned your lesson? It seems like you haven't. I don't know if they took it easy on you inside, but prison life will eat you alive. When I first went in, I had to establish myself just like you do on the streets on the outside. People came at me every day. In the yard. In the shower. With homemade shanks. I got sliced a couple of times. Hangings in the jail cells, and friends murdered. You want nothing to do with that life." I looked him up and down and saw the shame in his face. "You're not cut out for it. You wouldn't last when they send you to the hole. Where you're locked in, darkness and rats are coming out of the corners, and the cell smells like rancid piss. No, my friend, that's not what you want, I can assure you." I gave him a hard stare.

I watched his Adam's apple bob up and down as I delivered the day's sermon. "You have a point. By the way, you don't have to put me up or nothing. I have a little money for a place. I'm just waiting for this shit to blow over. You know?"

He rubbed the back of his neck as we entered the production warehouse. A few empty barrels of grain feed were standing in the back corner. The makeshift conveyer belt was dusty, and the rubber was worn out. I would need to replace it.

"You can help me in here for starters. I need to prepare for crop season and fix some fences around the property. It's not glamorous work, but it's a good, earnest living and will keep you busy." I shifted my gaze to him as the overwhelming smell of hay, crops, and grains permeated the warehouse.

"I can deal with this." Hector's face changed to one of hope.

Maybe my prison stint had a bigger purpose, after all. I set Hector to work on the back fences, which needed some attention.

"Okay, Hector. I have to drop Bella off at school. What you can't do just leave, and we'll work on it when I get back."

He saluted and took his tools to the back fence. I smiled, glad I was doing some good.

As I entered the main house, Bella was in the kitchen

with a cup in front of her. I saw the steam coming out and peeked into it. "What you got in there?"

She snubbed her nose at me in a cute way. "I have some tea. Grandma taught me how to make it."

"You know how to cook on the stove, and with the water?"

"Yes. I do." Her little lips blew on the hot drink, and she sipped cautiously. Her hair fell just below her shoulder blades. Long hair like her mother.

"You are amazing, Bella."

She threw her hands up. "I know! Daddy, I'm excited to go to school today. I'm going to take a picture of Moonlight for a show and tell."

"That's a good idea, baby. I like it." Nothing like a Bella in your life to lift your spirit. "When you finish that, Daddy is going to take you to school."

"Okay."

Bella finished her drink and grabbed her book bag from the couch.

"Okay, I'm ready to go, Daddy."

"All right, then, let's go." I touched my face. I had a little stubble, but nothing major. It's the way I liked it. I'd trimmed up my edges, so I looked respectable. I knew I didn't fit in with cookie-cutter society, and that was okay with me. I wore a plain white T-shirt, jeans, and my tan cowboy boots.

As we rode over to Bella's school, she hummed all the way. I was still mesmerized by the little girl. She and Amber were the reasons I'd vowed to stay out of trouble. I pulled into a parking spot right out front. Little people were everywhere, getting dropped off. I saw the moms kissing their daughters, and I wondered how it made Bella feel.

"You okay?"

"Yes. Just sometimes, I'm sad when I think that Mommy

doesn't bring me to school." She dropped her head, and I felt the pain hit my chest.

"It's okay to be sad, sweety. But don't stay sad. Mommy wouldn't want that. She's here with you, watching over you. Over us both. Give Daddy a hug."

Her delicate arms reached my neck, and she slapped a wet kiss on the side of my face. "I have to go now! My friend Carly is there."

I laughed at her resilience. Just as quickly as she was sad, she was happy again.

"Grandma is going to pick you up, okay? Daddy has some business. You're going to stay with Grandpa and Grandma."

"All right. I stay there a lot. We have fun. I beat Grandpa in puzzles. He gets mad."

"That's Grandpa for you."

Bella opened the door and bounced into the school doors, skipping in with her friend, Carly. I felt a little heavy in my heart. Bella had built a whole life without me in prison. Where did I fit now?

I rode back home and worked alongside Hector in the Merced heat. I had my own demons to work through. I wanted the time to pass quickly. My wish was answered as dusk set over Merced.

"Hector, let's pack up for the day. It's showtime."

"You sure I can't come? I mean, you're only going to watch, right?"

"I am, but I'm going to be close enough."

Hector jumped in. "I'm coming with you. This whole transaction is about me."

"You got your car? Follow my lead. Come on, we have to load up just in case."

We went to the barn, and I turned on the light. It seemed like the little pigeons had hatched as I could hear the squawking. I put my hand out as we entered the entryway of the barn.

"Wait here," I commanded.

I climbed the ladder and uncovered my arms supplies. I grabbed the long-range rifle and the case of bullets. I also grabbed the two semi-automatics.

I climbed down, and Hector was taken aback.

"Cowboy, you're packing heat like that?"

I gave one nod of my head. "You better believe it. I'm an Outlaw. When we go to war, we go in armed. Here, take the semi. You know how to use it?"

"Yes, I do. I've had a few shots at the gun range. I'm not a bad shot."

I eyed him warily. "It's different when you're faced with the situation, and you have to fire in real life."

"Have you?" He cocked his head to look at me as we stood with our weapons and the horses looking at us.

"Yes. Once. I shot a dude in the leg for non-payment. I regret that. Again, in my younger years. I'm too old to be doing that, and I have a daughter to think about."

"I understand. What's that long rifle you got?"

"It's a long-range sniper. We're going to be sitting high up. We got walkies. So if anything pops off and I can get a clear shot off, I will take it."

Hector put his hands on his head in despair, which let me know he didn't have a killer instinct.

"Best you stay out of a game you can't play, Hector," I warned.

"I guess so. This shit's freaking me out."

I smiled. "Then my job is done. Come on. It's getting late, and I need to check in with the guys."

Remnants of dust kicked up as a soft breeze blew onto the farm. As we talked and I got out the walkies from my back room, I looked at my watch. Seven o'clock.

"Let's go. We need time to set up on the hill. I got the binoculars packed."

"Okay, I'm ready." Hector's face was pale, and he was sweating even though it was cool.

"Okay, good. Let me show you how the Outlaws do it."

AMBER

"Can I see Warden Smith? I have an appointment with him this morning."

Another visit to USP Atwater, and it was fast becoming my second home. The office administrator behind the glass gave me a weary look. She looked worn down.

Warden Smith came out of the office, greeting me with a wide smile. "Amber, always a pleasure. Come through."

I followed Warden Smith to the back room and passed all the others working in the office. They all turned their heads to look at me. I'd been trying to organize this meeting for months with him.

We made it to a small meeting room, and the standard jug of water was on the table. Warden Smith hitched up his pants. "Can I get you a cup of coffee?"

"Yes, cream and one sugar," I replied in a business-like tone. My stomach led the way in letting me know that Warden Smith might have the hots for me. His gaze lingered a little too long for my liking.

"Coming right up. I will be right back."

Warden Smith left the office, and I breathed deep as I

spread out my evidence. I was here on prison reform business. Some of it was reinforced by Colt's stories of the conditions he'd faced. Warden Smith came back five minutes later with two cups full of hot liquid. I could smell the coffee beans. He placed the cup in front of me. He, too, had a stack of paperwork in front of him.

"So, Amber, how are you doing?"

I got comfortable in my seat. "I'm doing great, Warden. I've wanted this meeting for the longest time."

"I know. I'm glad we've gotten around to it. Let's talk about it. What do you have for me?" He slapped his knee.

"Well, I want to commend you first on how you run the prison in terms of problem-solving. If an issue arises in my dealings with you, you have been quick to correct it."

Stroke the ego first. Warden Smith poked out his chest with pride. "Thank you, Amber. Go on."

"Having said that, at USP Atwater, there is a significant increase in suicide in jail cells. Also, there is a marked increase in inmates with mental health conditions, who strike out by murdering other inmates. The conditions in solitary confinement are dismal, and prisoners are being exposed to toxic metals when they are working outdoors. This is my hope for USP Atwater." I slid across a pamphlet for Hawaiian jails that showed how clean and neat they were. It also showed the plethora of prison programs available.

Warden Smith belly-laughed "You can't be serious. Hawaii? These men are hardcore prisoners. They don't need a home away from home."

"Not all of them are, and if the plan is to reform them so that they don't re-offend, we have to at least give them the right environment to thrive and gain the skills to go back into society. Not all of the prisoners at USP are lifers," I said passionately.

"I see what you're trying to do. What would this do for us?"

"It would reduce the number of dead bodies in your cells. Reduce the paperwork. Allow you to gain more funding if you have a healthy prison, and allow you to ultimately place more money back in your pocket."

I waited for the warden to comprehend what I was saying. "Okay. What is your first step?"

I eased him into it. "Report the numbers and file a report to the federal government to apply for funding."

The warden tapped the side of his coffee cup impatiently. "Trust me, we have to report every quarter."

"I know, but now there is a new program with a loophole. Check this out. It's a lot of reading, but I've highlighted the sections and what you may be able to get. It also refers to the Prison Reform Act."

He raised his eyebrows in what looked to be respect. "This is impressive. You've done your due diligence."

I smiled broadly. "I work for the Department of Human Services. I have to."

He pushed the documents aside. "I've meant to ask you something for a while now."

Warden Smith was not an attractive man. His face was lined with pockmarks, and his belly protruded over his pants even though his legs were incredibly skinny. I said, "Warden, I have a keen interest in prison reform, and as you know, my brother was in here for a while."

"Yes, yes, I remember. Let's get past all that." He waved his hand as if directing traffic out of the way. "I wanted to know if you would like to have a drink with me sometime." He bared his teeth in a greasy smile.

"Uh. No, thank you, Warden. I appreciate the offer, but I have a boyfriend, and you have a wife."

The greasy smile remained. "Well, if that changes, just give me a call. You know where I am."

I balked and packed my things up. "Thanks, Warden. I have a busy day, so I'd better be going now."

"Okay. I do, too. See you soon, Amber." Warden Smith hitched up his pants and left the table. He swiftly opened the door. I walked past him, and I caught him closing his eyes, inhaling. I picked up the pace and headed for the outdoors. The guy made my skin crawl.

As I drove back to the office on my usual route, I mentally patted myself on the back. I'd done my best, and that's all anyone could hope for. Today was a half-day because the next day I would be in training for my new role. The other issue that hung around the back of my mind came to the forefront. Colt and Hector. They were going to settle things tonight. My head had been pounding with mortifying scenarios.

I grabbed the lavender-scented oil I carried in my bag for stress reduction and sniffed it. I let the velvety scent float into my nostrils and soothe me.

As I packed up, I saw Lucy's car leaving the parking lot. Another problem eliminated, at least for the day. Work went well and the day passed quickly.

I called Colt, wanting to hear that sexy, down-low, California cowboy accent. I peeked outside. I saw a few of my work colleagues heading to the coffee shop for their break. I waved, and they waved when they saw me.

"Hi."

"Hi, beautiful. Missing me, huh?"

I paused because I wanted to say something about what was coming. It hung in the air like the elephant in the room between us. "Yes, I am."

"How's your day?" he reached.

"As good as can be. How's Hector doing? Driving you bananas yet?"

"No. He just needs a little guidance. I see the route he's heading down. I'm going to turn that around for him if I can. He's a good kid."

"Colt? Be careful tonight. I don't want to talk about it or anything. I think I've said enough."

"I understand. I love you. It will be like nothing ever happened."

"Maybe. Maybe not. Just be careful."

"You think I'm going to let anything happen to me when I got your fine ass, Bella, and your brother out here? I'm not a stupid man."

"Bye, baby," I replied silkily.

"Bye, honey."

"Colt?"

"Yeah?

"I love you." I couldn't hold it in any longer.

A thick air of silence lingered for a moment.

"I love you, too, Amber."

COLT

The dark veil of the Merced night sky hung above our heads. Hector and I were on a hill, looking down on the Las Balas crew. My mental focus was sharp and my breathing even. When I was in the heat of the fire, I could stand like the courageous cowboy I was. We were early. Both of us were lying low on our bellies above the grassy knoll.

"Here, take a look. Do you know any of those Las Balas guys?"

I handed Hector the binoculars. I'd spotted three men in leather jackets, and all of them were smoking and shuffling around outside the abandoned warehouse on East Mission Road. The streetlight was the only illumination in the otherwise empty parking lot.

Hector was breathing heavily. "That's the prick that set me up in the deal in the first place. Rodrigo. That guy is a fucking worm. The other guys with him I don't know."

My long-range Twilight sniper rifle was set up on a mini tripod, and that thing could reach a target over ten thousand feet away. The Las Balas crew had no idea that we were within shooting range of them.

"Sounds about right," I said with a lowered voice. I peered through the lens. At this point, I had a clear shooting range of all three of the crew. Parked on the left-hand side was one lone SUV. All of them must have arrived together.

I had two walkie talkies sitting in between us in case Mikakov instructed that we needed to move. I'd managed to convince him that Hector needed to be present. They were on low volume. The men were standing outside an old abandoned, tin shed warehouse that used to be a gas plant. The main parking lot was out front with no other businesses surrounding it, just the wheat-colored fields of Merced. I scanned the perimeter with binoculars. Not a man or Las Balas crew member in sight.

I smirked in the darkness. "This is going to be good. They think you're showing up. Let's see what they do."

With my high-profile binoculars, I saw a crew member winding a silencer on the end of a gun. I handed the binoculars back to Hector.

"See, what did I tell you?"

He looked through the lens and saw what I saw.

"Shit. They were going to fucking kill me. I mean, what if I had the money? Would they still have killed me?" He handed the binoculars back.

"I guarantee you wouldn't have come out of this alive. They would have shot you dead. The Las Balas crew are a bunch of low-down, dirty rats."

The second guy also pulled his gun out, ready for action. They were cajoling and laughing with one another. All of these bitches were about to be rocked.

My walkie flashed angrily at me, and I picked it up, pressing the intercom button on the side.

"Go ahead," I whispered.

"You in position?" A thickly textured Russian accent came through.

"Roger that."

"Prepare. Watch the fields behind the warehouse."

"Done. Over and out."

We heard the blood-curdling sound before we saw it. A large black van swung around the parking lot corner, screeching to a halt. The Las Balas crew lifted their guns, primed for rapid-fire. The black van door ripped open, and the Russian boys leaped out. My mouth turned up into a huge smile. They jumped out like the ninjas they were. They were all dressed in black leathers, fully armed. I heard the raised voices of the Las Balas crew talking and swearing in Spanish.

"Mierda!" They shouted out, Tweedledee and Tweedledum waving their arms around and grabbing their guns.

I watched Mikakov raise his arms out wide. The Las Balas crew stopped moving and stopped talking. Both Hector and I were mesmerized by the showdown.

There was a heated exchange between the two. I know because I saw the veins lifted on Mikakov's neck. His team flanked him and raised their guns at one point. The icy night wind cut through the grass and across our faces, causing me to shiver involuntarily. The Las Balas crew members' faces looked shocked, and Mikakov beckoned one of his men, who reached in the van and brought out a suitcase.

The suitcase was opened, and I zoomed the binoculars in. It was the almighty greenbacks and lots of them. He closed the case and slid it over to them. One of the main henchmen pointed their gun to one of the others, gesturing for him to count it. Through the lens, I could see him rifling through the notes, counting. It took about ten minutes. Once satisfied, my man Mikakov gestured with a cut-your-throat motion and a gun-to-the-head motion. I knew what that meant.

I tapped Hector, encouraging him to see for himself. "Look. There it is. All clear."

Hector looked, his mouth dropping wide open. "Holy shit. You just saved my life. I can't fucking believe this. Are you sure they won't come after me?"

I could just make out his face in the night. "I'm sure. The Russians are not the men to play with."

"Okay," he said mildly.

I watched through the lens. The last of it was over. We could all move forward now. I watched the Russians wait until the Las Balas crew left. I saw the walkie flash again.

"It's over. Debt paid in full. We took care of it. With a few incentives for them not to try anything."

"Thanks, Mikakov."

"We owed you. Your loyalty has not gone unrecognized."

"Roger that."

"Tell Hector to stay the hell away from those fuckers."

"Will do. Over and out."

"You don't have to tell me twice. I want nothing to do with that life."

I slapped him on the back. "Come on, let's go."

Erring on the side of caution, we hung in the tall blades of grass for another twenty minutes. Then we both rose. My muscles were cramped from lying in position. Over the top of the hill and over the other side, my vehicle was parked. Two open fields, nothing but dusty California dirt and sparse grass that never had a chance to grow, separated us from the car. There were no streetlights on this side, just the glistening sliver of the luminescent moonlight. I listened for even the faintest sound of footsteps or anything funky. Nothing. My heartbeat quickened for some reason, thundering through my ears. The wind picked up.

Hector was in the car. The ebony night brought something wicked. The sound of someone running in the darkness. Sharp intakes of breath, gaining.

I reached for my gun. Dammit! I took it off my waistband

when we were all clear. Mikakov's warning rang in my ears. Watch the fields.

I stepped into the slice of the moonlight.

I saw a snarling face, ten paces away.

Don't get out of the car, Hector. Stay put.

I squatted to the ground, grabbing a handful of dusty brown dirt. I fisted it and threw it directly at the running target.

He stumbled back in shock, grunting. I caught the barrel of the pistol in his hand. Due to the shock, he stumbled to the ground. I kicked the gun away. I heard Hector get out of the car. On the rebound, so he didn't have time to recover, I swung back and engaged from the hip, delivering a body blow. I watched him fly back a few feet as I knocked the wind out of him. I was twice his size.

"Who the fuck are you?" I demanded.

The man fell back, and I straddled his face. He had on his leathers with the Las Balas crew logo. Hector tried to come in while the guy was discombobulated.

"No! Back."

The black van of the Russians came swerving into view. Mikakov swung out. "I told you to watch the perimeter. I knew it was too easy," he said.

He pulled the gun and shot a clean shot straight at the man's head. It all happened in a split-second flash. Hector faced away. Brain fragments soiled the dirt as the shiny, rich blood seeped from the hole in the man's head. I looked closer and saw he was definitely of Spanish descent.

Mikakov signaled with his gun, waving us off. "You two, go now! We clean up this mess." His angry Russian accent was enough to move us on from the site.

"Thanks."

I got inside the car, and we drove away in silence.

"Don't tell Amber. She doesn't need to know, okay?" I

heaved with a sudden sickening weariness resting on my shoulders. "You're safe now."

"Thanks, man, that shit was crazy." Hector's face was coming back to color. It had been white as a sheet earlier. It looked like it was the first time he'd seen a dead body.

"See why I didn't want you to come?"

Time for a fresh start.

AMBER

Two strong knocks rapped on my door just after ten o'clock at night. I didn't have a peephole. Anxiety weakened my voice.

"Hello?" I squeaked out.

"Hey, it's me. Colt."

I opened the door wide, and a tired, weary cowboy stood before me.

"Oh my God, what happened? You look terrible!"

He placed both of his large, now callused hands on both sides of my face and kissed with every bit of passion I think he had.

"I love you, Amber Atwood."

His clothes were drenched as I felt around his waist for injuries. There were none. I touched his right hand, and it was badly swollen. I focused on it.

"You're hurt. Sit down." I went to the fridge and grabbed one of the snap ice packs and a dish towel. I wrapped it around his fist. "Hold it in place," I commanded.

His face was laced with pain, and he gritted his teeth.

When he saw the worry on my face, he turned his wincing into a grin.

"I'm okay. Your brother is okay, too. He's at the house. I had to see you. I wanted to let you know I'm safe." He paused. "You have some alcohol? This is going to sting for a few hours."

"Sure. I have bourbon. I have—"

"Bourbon. That's the one. Neat. Thanks."

On my tiptoes, I reached for my special square tumblers. I brought the bourbon out of the alcohol cabinet, pouring the dirty brown liquid in the glass for him.

"Ice?"

"No. Just like that. Get ready for the re-up. This shit hurts."

I didn't take my eyes off him.

"Baby, I'm not going to pass out, if that's what you think. Plus, you ain't going to be able to lift me off the ground in a hurry." He chortled a little. I tried to hide the little smile creeping up, but he saw it. "There it is. I knew that smile was in there."

"Here, drink this and shut up," I commanded.

"Yes, ma'am." He tossed it back in one fell swoop.

"Another?"

"Yes." I poured him another one, and this time, I drew down a glass and poured myself one. I added ice.

"Joining in the party?" he asked spicily.

"Yes, I am. Now tell me what the hell happened out there. Why is your hand like that?"

He shifted to the couch and drove his muscular frame into it, dropping his head back. Fuming, I stood in front of him, demanding answers. My chest was heaving from anger, and I knew my cheeks were rosy. My hair most likely looked wild, but I didn't care. Neither did he.

His eyes turned to darkened, hungry desire. He reached

his long arms up under the length of my nightgown and cupped my butt, bringing me forward to his face. He pressed his head into my center, his non-injured hand roaming around near the softness of my belly, and my anger subsided, replaced with decadent longing. He pulled the waistband of my panties down swiftly. I threw my head back as I placed my hands on both of his shoulders. He stroked the opening where the lava ran. I felt like I was on a slippery slide of desire as his tongue did the work. I moaned out loud, gasping for air. A raging fire burned through my soul at his deft touch.

"Yes!" I cried out as the pressure of his hand increased. I watched the lusty greed on his face as he got turned on by my moans. He slipped my panties all the way off, and in a flash, he'd whipped off his underwear and his jeans to reveal his full erection.

"Sit right here." He demonstrated by putting his hands on his cock.

I obliged and sat down on him, my walls expanding with his thickness. I set a furious pace, letting the anger transmute into the fiery heat of a wild, wanton woman. I was riding him like the cowboy he was. He grabbed my bucking hips and quickened the process, grunting with elemental need. He smiled in the darkness at my urgency.

"Go, baby, keep going. I like it when you're angry."

His breathing was fragmented as he tried not to get his injured hand in the way. His shirt was still on, a tank. I shoved it over his head and threw it to the side as I rode. He kneaded my full, double-D breasts like kneading dough through my nightgown. I ripped it over my head to reveal them in full bounce. An orgasm crept up on me without warning, shattering me into small pieces of ecstasy.

He gave me the room to breathe and laid me carefully on the carpeted floor, hovering over me for a moment. "I love you."

"I love you, too. Now get down here."

Round two of the erotic dance began, and this time it was slower from him.

"Does your hand hurt?"

"I'm not worried about my hand right now, that's for sure."

I stroked his prominent jawline with the back of my hand. He lifted one of my legs to wrap around him, kissing me deeply. He found my promised land and controlled his rotation, sending me into slow, glorious torture. He ground his hips and continued to kiss my swollen lips. All it did was build an ache up bigger than California inside of me. He kept the same pace, driving me nuts.

"Babe, you're killing me—in a good way. Please," I called out.

"You sure?" he breathed. He knew he had me right where he wanted me. I felt his thick muscular arms straining as I dug into his tightly defined chest.

"Yes!"

My body started to grip and tighten around him. I felt the second wave of orgasm hit. The carnal grind of his hips picked up as I felt him swelling inside me. The heat between us caused his Adonis-like body to become glossy with sweat. I grabbed his head and drew it down to my lips. I wanted to experience what he was feeling. He released a guttural moan into my mouth as he came. His body became slack as I reached around his back to hug him, then he rolled to the side.

"Make-up sex is not so bad after all," he panted.

COLT

I woke up to a throbbing hand and a mouthful of hair. I swiped the hair from my face. It was Amber's long, luxurious mane of glory. I rolled over to face her. She had rolled onto her side and was sleeping soundly. I admired her curvature and the groove of her back. I ran my finger down her spine to her round buttocks. She was all woman—a heavenly sight to wake up next to for me. The peace she exuded made me calm. I rolled on my back and examined my hand. Not too bad, but it still hurt like a motherfucker. I flexed to check the range of movement. It should be back to normal within the week as long as I iced it. I stretched out from top to bottom, looking around to check out Amber's room. I saw a closet on the left-hand side, two bedside drawers, a few big teddy bears in the corner, and a desk with girly things on it—perfumes, bracelets, and earrings.

We were lying right under a large window, and the early light was streaming through. I moved my large frame from the bed and into the kitchen. Her curtains were drawn, and I could see the magnificent view she had. It looked right out over the back of the mountains. I could just make out the faint outline of them. My mind flashed back to last night and that the Russians killed a man in front of Hector. There was no chance of him snitching because it involved him. The reason we were there was because of him.

I rummaged through the cupboards to look for coffee or tea. I wanted to make one for Amber before she got up. I knew she had to go to work. I eventually found what I was looking for.

My mother would say I did a *man look* if I couldn't find something. I shook my head when I thought about her. I was eternally grateful for her support. She was a rock. I put the water on the stove and let it boil. I placed two cups down from the cupboard and filled both with a teaspoon of instant coffee. I knew Amber liked sugar in hers, so I pried open one of her canisters and added some.

I heard a yawn and soft feet coming around the corner. A very sleepy and cute Amber came into the kitchen with a bedsheet wrapped around her. I opened my arms wide for her to enter. With a dopey smile, she fell into my arms and laid her head on my chest. I ran my hand through her tangled web of thick blond hair.

"I know. I know, it needs a good brushing." She smoothed her hair down over my fingers, still leaning into my chest.

"No. I like it. I should be able to brush it for you. I brush my horse's tails."

She looked up then to my wide grin, lightly tapping me on the chest. "Did you just call my hair a horse's mane?"

"Yes, I did. But not in a bad way. I love it. Your hair is so thick, that's all. It's luscious like you." I touched her soft lips with mine. As she kissed me back, the water boiled. She released me as I poured her coffee and handed it to her.

"Thank you, sweety. How is your hand today?"

"It's a lot better. Thank you."

She took the first sip of her coffee and scanned me up and

down. I had my jeans back on and was shirtless. "Hot damn, you look good in the morning. I look a mess," she exclaimed in mock disgust.

"You don't at all. You look like a sexy siren," I assured her.

She blew the steam off her coffee. "I think I'll keep you. You're good for my self-esteem."

I laughed at her, kissing her on the head. "Going into work today?" I asked.

"Yes. Back to saving the world."

I rubbed her back. "I have a lot to do today. Bella is back from her grandma's, your brother is working with me, and I have to go clear up some other things."

It seemed like she only heard me say *other things*. "What other things?" She walked to the kitchen table and sat down.

"Just fixing up some things from last night. Nothing you need to be concerned about."

I sat my cup of Joe on the counter. I didn't know if I would have time to drink it.

"You're never going to tell me about last night, are you?"

"You don't need to know, Amber. Plus, you've done enough for me."

"You saved my brother's life, Colt. So I think it's the other way around," she said quietly.

"It's nothing to me and easily solved. I'm going to hit the shower and get ready."

"Okay."

I dove into the shower and washed off the remnants of our lovemaking. I came out fresh and squeaky clean, ready to handle whatever the day threw at me. I kissed Amber goodbye and left, thinking that after all the battles I'd endured, maybe things were turning around for the long term.

I pulled up to the house and noticed Hector was already at the front fences, slogging away.

"Hey, you're hard at it already. You good out here? It's pretty hot."

"Yeah, I could use a glass of water." He wiped his brow. It looked like he was trying to shake off last night.

I went inside and grabbed a bottle of water for him and one for me. I switched over to my cowboy boots and took him the water.

"Hey, brother. Stop for a minute." As he gulped the water down, I studied him. I squinted from the heat picking up. "You worried about that guy last night?"

"No, and yes. I mean, I've seen someone overdose. I've seen a person die before, but not like that. I don't know, it was kind of scary."

I nodded my head solemnly. "Like I said, you ain't cut out for that lifestyle. What you saw was a scumbag being eliminated. If he wasn't shot, he would have killed you or me."

Hector twisted his lips as he thought about it. "Yes, I know. He came out of nowhere, though. How did we not see him?"

I shrugged my shoulders. "I mean, who knows? He was probably lying down in the grass like we were on the hilltop."

"I guess," he mumbled.

"You check the horses?"

"Yep. Sure did. That Moonlight is a hell of a horse."

I swatted away the flies from my face. "She sure is. Hey, I want to take you somewhere today. I want to give you some extra backup."

"Backup?"

I looked at him again. "Yes. I want you to meet my brothers in the MC, The Outlaw Souls."

"Ah, okay. Are we headed there now?"

"No time like the present," I claimed.

"Okay. Sounds good."

I went inside to grab my keys, and we drove over to where

the trouble started. This would be my first time seeing all the boys in action. I pushed the ugly monster of fear back down. We came up to a large warehouse with a parking lot in the back. It had a few neighboring businesses, but not many.

As we parked, I saw Diego with his long hair and greasy towel come to the front of the warehouse. He was there with a few of the other Outlaw Souls members. Vlad happened to be there, too. He was puffing on a cigarette, looking like the Grim Reaper himself.

I looked over at Hector as we approached, and he looked like a scared little rabbit.

Vlad gave me a hard handshake, and Diego brought me in for a warm hug. Two very different men, but brothers nonetheless.

"Hey, hey, if it isn't Mr. Cowboy himself!" Diego gave me his big rosy smile, a refreshing change from all these diabolical, hard-nosed criminals.

"It's me."

"Glad to hear you're out now," Diego said, looking hard at Hector.

"Hey, guys, I want you to meet Hector. He's with me. I wanted to bring him in so he could check out the bikes and see how it's done, Diego."

Diego smiled and summoned him in. "For sure. Any friend of Colt's is a friend of mine."

I walked a step behind with Vlad. He spoke out the side of his mouth. "If you want back in, just say the word."

"No. Never again." I clenched my jaw hard. I was pissed that he was even asking me. Vlad's cold eyes surveyed me. The guy was pure darkness.

"All right, all right. The operation is much smoother now. We are, you know, doing some things a little differently." He moved his hands side to side like a weighing scale.

I sneered as we walked over to the bikes resting on the

platform station. "I've heard that before. No, no. I'm good now, Vlad. Number one, my girl would kill me. Second of all, I did my time. Third, I'm focused on running the farm. Ryder offered me a job here to work with Diego, but given the way Diego and Hector are hitting it off, this might be his gig."

I nodded at both of them getting on like a house on fire. Hector was talking in an animated fashion and making all kinds of noises.

"You're right. I commend you, and we will be forever in your debt for not snitching. If you need anything, you call," Vlad responded.

"I will, brother."

"Much respect, Colt." He put a fist to his heart. "I have to slip out. I have errands to run." He didn't give me time to respond. The master of darkness, as I liked to call him, slipped away without saying goodbye. I watched his black Jeep ride out.

I returned my gaze back to look at the lineup of bikes. Diego had come a long way from the beginning of opening the Merced chapter. He had three regular guys working in the shop with him, and ten bikes were in front of us, all of them ranging from dirtbikes to choppers to crotch rockets.

"Hector, what do you think?" I asked.

"I'm freaking out right now. That's the new Ducati. Custom painted. Man, I wish I knew how to fix these beasts. I mean, I got a basic bike, but these puppies are next level."

"You're in your element, I see."

I signaled to Diego. Hector had no idea, as he was busy checking out the chrome detail on the bikes.

"Hey, man, do you think you could take him under your wing, in terms of the shop? Teach him some things?" My voice was lowered from the earshot of Hector.

Diego didn't hesitate. "Yes. I need an extra pair of hands, and he can help out on the paperwork, too. I'll teach him the ropes. Leave the kid with me. We're legit here. I don't know what Vlad told you, but I wouldn't even think about heading back that way with him. Never was you, Colt." He tapped me on the back. "I know you were trying to get money for the family, so I respect it. Stick to your horses."

"I hear you. I'm not anxious to go back to that hellhole any time soon."

"Good. Let me talk to him." Diego winked. "Hey, young man. How about you come work with me? We got some rides going on, too. We head up to Yosemite sometimes. What do you think about that? Twenty dollars per hour as a trial, and as you get better, I'll raise the salary."

"Are you serious? Isn't this supposed to be Colt's gig?" He looked at me

"This is your gig, brother. I'm happy for you. You're a better fit for it. Follow your passion."

"Well, shit, then hell yeah, I'm in! Thanks!"

Watching Hector beam with excitement made me realiz that I wasn't following my own passions. That had to change. I had an idea, but I needed to run it past Bella first.

"Hey, now you know where your new workplace is, you can come here and start. I have to go pick up Bella."

Hector dapped Diego. "Thanks for the opportunity. When do I start?"

"You can start tomorrow if you want. It's up to you. Or you can come at the start of next week. I'll put you on the books right away."

Hector put his hands on his head. "No, I'm going to come tomorrow. Better I start sooner rather than later."

The balance of life was slowly being restored.

AMBER

"Still sleeping with the cowboy?"

My mug slipped from my fingers, but luckily, it was on a carpeted floor. The caramel-colored liquid contained in the cup flew out, staining the rug.

Lucy held her throat with her fat little fingers, laughing so hard I thought she was going into a spasmodic fit.

"What the hell is wrong with you? Why do you keep saying that?" I bit back at her with force. We were in the breakroom by ourselves, which was unusual there, as there was usually someone trying hard to escape their cases or gossiping at the water cooler.

"Because I saw you kissing him outside the grocery store. I knew from the glow up you had when you got back from the prison." My mouth was agape, and I had a hard time pulling it back shut. "Oh, don't worry, honey. Your secret is safe with me. I've had a jailbird a time or two. Lots of fun, isn't it?"

I grabbed a rag from the kitchen and cleaned up the coffee as best I could. "I don't know what you're talking about, Lucy, and I'm not sure who you saw, but it wasn't me."

My feeble attempts to cover up were not working in my favor. She narrowed her eyes at me.

"Come on now. You're only fooling yourself. But if that's what you want to do, it's all good. We got training today?" She switched the subject.

"Yes, we do at eleven."

"I'll see you then." She winked and carried herself back to her desk.

As I retreated back to my desk, I checked over my paperwork. I pulled up Colt's file. Now the visits would back off because Bella was back in her father's care. I made some notes and finalized my report. Technically, I was due to see Bella in six months to check in. A wry smile lifted on my face because I knew I would be seeing Bella in a couple of days. I daydreamed about my future with Colt. We hadn't really talked about it, though. I presumed he would start back up on the farm. It dawned on me that I didn't really know where I stood with him.

How would I fit into his life? Was he over the death of his late girlfriend? Even as his social worker, I was supposed to ask him these questions. I guessed that my primary concern was making sure Bella was okay. My big, strong cowboy didn't talk so much about those types of things.

I checked the time on my computer. In just over an hour, I had a meeting with my new team to discuss their cases. Usually, the team meetings consisted of discussing caseloads and providing tips back and forth about what to do. Unprecedented cases would filter through the team supervisor, which was me now. My stomach churned a little from the unknown of the job and if I would be able to handle the tougher, more disturbing cases. My specialty was those incarcerated, but the child cases caused me a lot of distress. I eyed the pile of paperwork in my end tray, all documents to do with training a team and case files that were tricky. Sometimes, all I wanted to do was float away from it all. My mind was telling me that maybe I wanted to do something that was less taxing on my physical and mental health. All I saw was a crossroads.

I packed up my things and prepared for the meeting, set on the agenda for twelve seats. People from our team streamed in and took their seats.

"Hi, Marsha, welcome to the meeting."

"Hi, Brandon, great job on that Hernandez case and getting it into the children's court."

Brandon wiped his brow. "Yeah, that was a tough one. Nearly broke my heart."

"I hear you. Some of these cases can do that."

"Lucy."

"Amber. Sit anywhere?" She had this devious smile on her face, and my shoulders knotted together as soon as she entered the room. The remainder of the group came in, and I shut the door.

"Hi, everyone. I'm glad that you could take time out of your days to join me for the meeting. I wanted to let you know I am now in charge of overseeing your cases. Michelle has moved on to a higher role." I looked around at their faces, and no one appeared disgruntled at the announcement, except for Lucy. "I can proudly say I have worked with each and every one of you in some capacity. It has been an absolute joy to do so. We can't save everyone, but I know that all of you try your best. That's all we can do."

"We're glad you're here. You're a wealth of knowledge," Brandon said.

"I second that," Cynthia, one of the longest-standing members of the department's team, chimed in.

"So, I know we have an agenda, but let's just open the floor. Do any of you have any problems with your current cases? Let's help one another out. We can go around the room."

Lucy put her hand up. My legs were crossed, but I squeezed them together, invisible to the others.

"Yes, I have a question." Her eyes danced with mischief.

"Go ahead, Lucy. You have the floor," I answered curtly.

"What happens in a misconduct case? Such as if a social worker or department worker becomes involved with a client?" My heart stomped through my chest. My palms were sweating. I maintained my cool as best I could.

"Well, first, that's a serious allegation, and you would need undeniable proof that something was going on. Remembering that we, as social workers, are involved with home visits and accessing certain services to assist our clients. You would need proof for such a claim, and then the next necessary steps would be taken." My caramel eyes inflicted my coldest stare back at her.

She smiled. "Just wondering is all." She rolled her eyes arrogantly.

Brandon sat forward in his seat. "Why do you ask? Do you know someone in that position, Lucy?"

She looked straight at me, and I maintained a neutral if not blank stare. "Oh God, no, no one from this team would do that!"

A few of the others mumbled under their breath before the meeting continued. Maybe Colt and I might need to cool it until compulsory visits were over. I didn't want to jeopardize him or me. The meeting overall was productive and ended after forty-five minutes. The threat of blackmail from Lucy had me thinking vengeful thoughts. I had the opportunity to confront her as she was the last to leave out of the room.

"What exactly are you doing? I mean, what exactly are you trying to prove? Did I miss something?

Lucy's dark eyes lit up with envy as she looked at me. "Yes, you can do no wrong in this department. You're a goody-two-shoes, and I'm sick of it. You got that promotion, and I'm just as qualified as you for the role. In fact, I've had just as many cases as you."

The root cause of the conflict was revealed. I blew out a strong breath. "Look, your time is coming. I don't know why you would be in a hurry for the role. Better the devil you know. I work late nights, and up until now, I haven't really had a life outside of helping other people. Think about it."

Her energy shifted slightly, but she'd already decided to be mad. "Well, I want to hate you, but you make it hard to." She cracked a smile.

I took the high road and flashed her one back. "See, not so bad after all. I will do my best to give you some cases that can get you to the next level. Would you consider another branch?"

Lucy's eyes widened. "Now you're trying to send me away?"

"No, actually, I might have something for you. But you have to lay off."

She heaved a sigh. "Okay, I could use the extra money. My mother's having a heart transplant next month."

The lightbulb flashed, and the sudden change in demeanor became clear. "Give me some time. I think I can create a role you'd like."

COLT

The smell of the sweet California grass had me in a good mood. My girl Bella and I were in the barn. Both of us were feeding the horses and cleaning up. I stared at the clumps of pigeon poop as I looked down at the barnyard floor. The pigeons had formed their little nest at the top of the barn attic. I found it surprising, as normally they liked caves. These cute little gray fluffy babies caught my eye from time to time.

Bella loved them. The chickens were another story. I had to shoo them away from time to time because they were a little too curious. I watched her as she hummed and fed the Palomino horses hay. They chomped happily and neighed back, the horses' version of talking.

"Daddy, I think we should name the little birds." Right after she said it, a little fluff ball wobbled on its little legs next to Bella, desperately trying to flap its wings and fly. He couldn't fly yet.

I pointed behind her feet. "Well, there's the first one. Name that one."

She turned around, and I thought the chick might try to

fly away, but it didn't. It stayed put. Bella picked it up in her tiny hands and peered at it. To my surprise, it tucked its wings in and sat peacefully in her hands. Not only a horse whisperer but an animal whisperer.

"Let's call you Flappy because you flap your wings a lot, trying to fly."

I arched an eyebrow at her, and Moonlight raised her nose in approval, stomping the ground.

"Oh, you approve, do you?" I fed her a carrot, and her large teeth made quick work of it. Nearly took off a few of my fingers, but I managed to get them out of the way fast enough.

Bella petted the chick with two small fingers, and it chirped as well as it knew how. After a little while, she put it down. The mama pigeon swooped down and bobbed its neck back and forth around the chick. She led her little one away from us humans. Maybe she was worried her chick would get trampled.

I stroked Moonlight's nose, and she butted my hand. She knew in my other hand, I had an apple, which was a little trickier to feed her. I wanted to keep all my fingers.

"Bella, can I ask you something?"

"Sure, Daddy. What is it?"

"What do you think about building an arena out here? Maybe we could teach people to ride."

She sucked in air and spun around, her brown ponytail swinging with her. "That's a great idea, and I could make new friends!"

"I might need to get a couple more horses later, but we could start small. We have that trail back out here."

"I want you to do it. That sounds like fun."

I put my hand out flat and let Moonlight take the apple. She stomped her hoof in her stable, her beautiful mane flicking across the bridge of her nose.

"Moonlight likes the idea, too," Bella said.

I looked carefully at the horse. "I don't think Moonlight will be the one to ride. She's too wild. Only you, Grandma, and I can ride her. She's very selective about people."

Bella giggled as she hugged my leg. I ran my fingers over the top of her hair.

"No." Bella shook her head at me.

"No to what?"

"Grandma can't ride her. She doesn't ride anymore, remember?"

I stopped for a moment.

"Yes, I do remember. I'm just so used to her riding. She was pretty good on horseback in her day."

Moonlight was eyeing me, hoping for more snacks, but I had none to give.

Bella twisted her hair in her hands. "Really? She seems to like baking cookies now. That's all she does."

Bella swung in a circle, making herself dizzy. She plummeted to the barnyard floor from the spinning. In examining my daughter, for once, I felt content. Everything was coming together for Bella and me. I touched my pants pocket. My phone was vibrating, and I answered it without looking at the screen.

"Hello, Colt speaking," I answered.

"So professional." Instantly, I worked out it was Amber.

"Hi, sweetness. How's my girl?"

"Colt, why are you keeping things from me?" She wasted no time being angry. I just didn't know what about.

I glanced over at Bella. She was dancing around the barn, and the horses were watching her. "Tell me why you're upset, baby. I don't understand."

"Why didn't you tell me that you would get Hector a job with the same club that sent you to prison?"

I sighed with relief. "I can clear that up. I planned to tell you when I saw you. Diego runs the motorcycle repair shop, and your brother loves bikes. It's the perfect fit for him. He and Diego got on like a house on fire. Diego wants to teach him about bikes. It will keep him out of trouble."

"I don't know. I don't want the cops bringing any more heat to him or you. He's on parole just like you."

"You have to trust me more. Diego is not involved with the illegal side of the business. That's Vlad and his Russians. Diego has nothing to do with that."

"It doesn't matter. He is affiliated with the club and its name. I really don't know how I feel about the situation."

My moment of contentment was fleeting, it seemed. "Baby, I'm willing to take Hector under my wing. I will look out for him."

I heard her sigh through the phone in discontent. "I'm sorry. I'm just trying to process everything. So much is going on, and we're up against so much. Sometimes I don't know what to do, that's all."

"I know it's hard, but I have an idea about something. I want to run it past you. Will you come for dinner tonight? Please? I need to kiss that beautiful face of yours," I replied with softness.

"Yes, but it better be good, Colt."

"It is. You're going to want to be involved, too. Let's give us a chance. Give it some time. You'll see the man I am."

AMBER

My insecurities were flaring up. It seemed like every time I tried to move forward with Colt, something popped up that made me question him. I wanted to trust him implicitly.

I pulled my hair up into a ponytail and put on jeans and a black top, ready to head to Colt's house. As I got ready, I put on some music to decompress from the day.

I'd made some calls to Merced USP that day.

"Warden Smith, have you looked into any information I gave you?"

"Well, I have. I see that it can work. There's a federal grant that would be ideal if we could swing it. We could look at upgrading a few things. I just don't have the administrative manpower to do it."

"That's why I'm calling. What about a prison liaison? Someone to help you in that department? An advocate for the jail, on a paid basis, of course."

"Let me think about it. I'll get back to you. They would have to guarantee a result if I paid them. I only have a small kitty of funds."

"Have a think about it and let me know."

I was thinking I might be able to get a job and a pay raise for Lucy to help her with the situation with her mother. I sighed as I applied my makeup. I was just about ready to go when I saw Hector's phone number.

"Hey, little bro! How are you?"

"I'm good. My head is spinning, though. I'm learning a lot at the repair shop."

"Okay, that's good news. Please tell me you're not shipping any illegal parts or anything like that."

"You have to trust Colt. He put his life on the line for me that night. Man, that guy would have killed us." He stopped short like he'd revealed too much.

"What...what did you say?"

"Nothing, Amber. Just leave it alone. It's done now. Diego is legit. Colt is legit. You don't have any reason not to trust him."

My belly was burning. I knew he wasn't telling me something. In a way, I wanted to know, and in another, I didn't. I eased out a breath and decided to let it go.

I drove over to Colt's and rapped on the door. As soon as I saw his face, I melted into mush.

"Hi."

One look is all it took with him. He scooped me up and into him. He planted a kiss on me that made me lift one foot off the ground, just like the movies.

"Baby. You mad at me?" His soulful eyes searched mine for the answers.

"A little, but I think I might be getting over it quickly."

He grabbed my hand and kissed it. "Come in, it's chilly out there."

"A little."

Bella ran into the room when she heard me open the door. She beamed like the ray of sunshine she was.

"Hi, Bella. How are you?"

She placed her hand in mine and led me to the kitchen table. Colt watched as we interacted.

"Glass of wine? I'm cooking tonight," Colt said.

"Wow. You are? What's on the menu?"

He grinned a little. "Well, we'll keep it kid-friendly. Uh. Don't get too excited. It's an easy meal. Homemade pizza."

"That sounds delicious. My favorite kind. Do you want any help?"

"You can pick your toppings if you want. Both you and Bella."

Colt had a plethora of options in little bowls on the open island bench. Mushrooms, bell peppers, pepperoni, ham, pineapple, cheese, chicken pieces, chilies, and a few others.

"I'm going to have the chicken, BBQ sauce, and mushrooms," Bella said proudly.

"Is that all you want on your pizza?" Colt asked.

"Yes. That's all I want. I love BBQ sauce," Bella replied. Her mind was made up.

"Okay then, little trooper. Simple pizza for you, coming up."

Colt wrapped his well-toned arm around me and kissed my lips softly. The bristles of his lightly stubbled chin tickled my face.

"I'm going to have ham, pineapple, mushrooms, and bell peppers," I confirmed with a smile.

"Okay, we got a loaded pizza. I'm going to have a pepperoni pizza. I'm a simple man."

It was nice to see this sexy hunk of a man performing the most domestic duties. I found it to be a huge turn-on.

"Okay, you have to leave the kitchen. You have to get out of here." Colt swiped the dish towel at Bella and me.

"Okay, okay. I'm leaving, Chef." I conceded with my hands up.

He laughed, and so did Bella and I. It was these little

blissful moments that led me to believe maybe we would be okay.

"Bella, can I ask you something?" I thought with the subject I was about to broach, it was best to just rip the Band-Aid off. "How do you feel about your father and me being friends?"

Her warm eyes looked at me for a while, and she smiled a little. "I like it. Daddy is happy when you're here, and you like horses, so it's fine by me. Grandma told me that you would be a good woman for Daddy."

Shocked and delighted at the admission, I found the conversation proved to be less painful than I had thought. Bella skipped off to her room, and I realized that Colt had heard every word.

"She loves you like I do," he said. "I'm glad you asked her, though. I'm not that good at that stuff sometimes."

I matched Colt's penetrating gaze. "You're better at it than you think you are. Sorry that I snapped about Hector earlier. It just took so much to get him out of trouble that I don't want him getting in it again."

"No need to apologize. I get it. We can work things out. In fact, I want to run something by you. I think I want to start a riding stable here. I think I want to teach people to ride. I might get a couple of older horses."

"Colt! That's a magnificent idea. Where did you come up with it?"

Colt had finished with the pizzas and put them in the oven. Now we were just waiting. I sipped my wine and relaxed a little.

"Bella. She has a way with the horses that I've never seen before. I want to live a clean life, and I decided not to take up the offer at the repair shop. I know Hector's there, but it's not the same as me being there."

"Okay. So you were willing to put my brother on the line and have him looked at?"

"Whoa. No. I offered Hector a job here on the farm, but when I saw him with Diego, I knew it was where he belonged. I belong on the land, Amber. I used to work with horses in my younger days." Colt pointed to the shelves. "You've seen the pictures."

I sighed. "Yes, I have. And I know you're right. Hector has loved bikes since he was a little boy. I do know this." I drank a little more.

Colt crossed the room in big strides. "This goes back to trust. I would never put Hector in danger intentionally."

"Forgive me. It's going to take me a little time to adjust, is all. I believe you, Colt."

COLT

Once my mind was made up, it was made up. I stood in the middle of the paddock next to the house. In ankle-length grass, I squatted down to feel the soil underneath. Hard California dirt. I had a ride-on mower, so I could cut it low in no time. The trick was how I was going to turn it into an arena. I needed local government permits to run a stable. That would be easy enough. My mind was sifting through what the next steps were.

"What do you think, son?" My father was standing beside me in a rare appearance. He'd become a couch potato over the years.

"It's going to be a lot of work, that's what I think. But I have this feeling in my bones that it will work."

"Son, I think it's a brilliant idea. That trail right there runs all the way to the mountain, and there are a couple of waterfalls back there, too. Unchartered territory. I'm proud of you. It takes a lot to get me out of the house these days, but this is a challenge I like. I'm going to map out these fence posts. Have you got the requirements yet?"

"No, not yet. Tomorrow. Okay, let's get to it then."

My father was a man of action, and still in decent shape in his late sixties.

I walked down to the production part of the warehouse and dusted off the riding mower. I fed her with some gas and rode back up to the paddock next to the house.

"Get it as low as you can. You might need to do two runs over it," my father said.

"That's what I thought, too."

I put on the earmuffs that were attached to the ride-on, started her up, and mowed circularly. It brought a smile to my face to have Dad here, working side by side. It felt like the old days when I was a kid and we had a few horses. As I looked at my dad measuring out the fences, it brought back memories.

"Now, son, this is the first time on the horse. You don't need to break them like they tell you. You just need to develop a relationship with them," he had told me.

That was a great day. It was my first day on a horse named Duncan. Duncan was a special horse. He was white with brown splotches all over him. Everybody loved Duncan, and he was the horse I won many events with.

I remembered crying in the barn when Duncan got old and passed away. He had been with me for twenty years of my life. I rode him every day. My father found me in there, curled up with my knees to my chest.

"It's okay, Colt. Sometimes people or things are taken from you because you don't need them anymore. Duncan's spirit is still here. Never forget that. I bet you, right now, he's stealing apples out of somebody else's hand up there in horse heaven."

"You think, Dad?" I wiped the salty tears from my face.

"I know, son."

Now here my father was, whistling and dancing as he put down markers for the fence. He was a man of the land, and I'd gladly followed in his footsteps. Every now and then, I thought of Charlie. We made good progress for the day, and my chest swelled with pride at the accomplishment.

"Bella coming with us tonight? We have a standing date to play cards."

"You're teaching my baby girl to be a card shark?" I squeezed my father's shoulder.

"Nope." His old eyes twinkled with a spark as we walked back to the house. "I'm teaching her how to read people and pay attention to her surroundings. It's a valuable lesson." My father waggled his finger.

"Yes, it is, Pop. I think Mom is picking her up from school today."

"Good. She beat me a little too quickly last time."

"Sounds about right for Bella. She's a smart cookie."

"That she is, my boy."

We'd started when the sun rose, and we were finished when the sun went down. The paddock now looked like an oval that you could run on. The fence posts were standing in position, ready for the next stage.

"Thanks, Pop, for your hard work today. It's shaping up."

"Yes, it is. Don't you let anyone else touch that fence. I'm the best man for the job. Nobody can build a fence like I can," he proclaimed defiantly. "Make sure you get those measurements. When I drop Bella off, I will finish it."

"Okay, Pop, sure thing."

I waved as he got in his old Pontiac and drove off. The mauve skyline of Merced let me know it might be time for a stiff drink. Before I had time to open the front door to the main house, a single gunshot rang out. I heard the horses neigh in alarm.

My heart lurched in my chest. Instincts kicked in. A weapon was needed.

I burst through my unlocked door and ran blindly to the

bedroom. I picked up my semi-automatic. I checked, and it was locked and loaded.

Nobody messed with my horses. I ran down to the barn with my breath raised to a frantic pace. Ten paces from the barn, the gravel crunching under my boots, I slowed. I closed my eyes and gritted my teeth, then I opened the side door to the barn.

I flicked on the light. There in the middle of my fucking barn was a Spanish man who resembled the man the Russians had shot. He had to be from the Las Balas crew. Sweat was dripping off him profusely. I sized him up. He was solid in build, but I could take him. He wore all black from head to toe. Trademark Las Balas. He had slicked back greasy dark hair and an olive-skinned complexion. I could make out the long scar on his neck. He was staggering like he was drunk or on drugs, one of the two.

"You might have gotten my brother, but you didn't know about me. Your fucking Russians couldn't catch me." His Spanish accent was thick, but I made it out and put two and two together, The now dead man wasn't alone in the field that night. I stilled my breathing and assessed the scene. He'd shot one of the Palominos, and he was crying out.

With nerves of steel, I said to him, "So what are we doing here? You shot my horse, motherfucker."

He threw his head back and laughed, his rotten teeth gleaming in the barn light.

"I'm a hard one to kill. Don't you know that? They call me Hosea. You're lucky I didn't gut your horse."

My Palomino was bucking and screaming with wild eyes. I could see him out of my peripheral, and it felt like someone had stabbed me in the heart a million times.

"What do you want?" I gritted through my teeth.

"Your blood in a bottle so I can take it back to my boys."

I let out a deathly laugh. "That shit ain't happening."

I moved sideways and stepped one pace to him. He followed my steps. My muscles flinched, coiled and ready for action. My semi-automatic was loaded, and we were both pointing at one another.

"Put your gun down, and let's fight fair. Man to man. You're on my property. Let it be a fight to the death," I said.

"Okay. You lower your gun, and I'll lower mine."

I knew what to do. Sure as the sun shone brightly in the morning. I knew what the hell I was going to do. "Let's go then. On the count of three. One."

He brought his gun down slightly. My eyes stayed unblinking, assessing his movements. They were rigid. His reflexes were off, almost like he was on drugs. I had him right where I wanted him.

"Two," I shouted out, and we lowered even further. The pace of my heart elevated and beats flooded one after the other in my chest. He sniffed. Both of us were wide open. I solidified my feet. "All right, you ready?"

"When you are, motherfucker."

"Three." I gritted my teeth, dropping like lightning on one knee, twisting my torso to line up with his feet, and raising my gun. I squinted with one eye, aiming for the ankle. Clear shot.

Bang!

Target hit.

"Son of a bitch!" He crumbled like a house of cards and fell down, lopsided. He rolled around in pain. "You shot me, you piece of shit."

Amber was standing shellshocked behind me with her mouth covered.

"Stay back!" I yelled. She heard the horse crying as she put the picture together. She fumbled with her phone.

The guy tried to move when he saw her with the phone at the barn door.

"No, you don't, you piece of shit." I kicked the gun out of his hand, and it slid across the barn.

"Yes. Roberts Crescent, please hurry. There's an intruder here. Yes, he has a gun." Amber was on the phone with the cops.

I kicked the Las Balas gang member in the teeth. I watched as his face ricocheted, and blood shot out of his mouth from the blunt force trauma of my cowboy boot. His face slumped to the ground, and his eyes began to roll.

"Son of a bitch shot my horse," I murmured. I didn't dare turn around. I yelled to Amber at the barn door, and she knew not to come any closer to the scene. "Amber, I need you to go to the first aid kit in the house and bring it here. Call my father. The number is on the fridge. Don't worry, baby."

"Okay, Colt." Terror reigned in her voice. I heard the quick pace of her feet. I knew she was running to the house as fast as she could.

A pool of thick blood was running from the man's ankle. I looked at the wound. I could see the meat of his ankle. I'd shattered it. Served the turd right.

I kicked him in it for good measure. He yelled out like a baby. "Please, spare my life. Don't kill me."

"Shut the fuck up!" I spat with anger. "I should have killed you the first time, but you're going to die a slow and painful death in jail. Oh yeah, because I got some boys that are going to play real nice with you inside. How about that?" I got down close to his ear. "Congratulations, you're about to become somebody's bitch."

It took the cops a whole eight minutes to reach us, and a crew of six cops came into the barn with their guns raised.

"Step back from him, Colt. We got it from here."

The boys in blue took in the scene, slapping the cuffs on the Spanish guy, but not before bandaging up his leg.

I lowered my gun. Another officer signaled for it. "Hand it over, Colt."

Limp armed, I handed over the gun to him. He had gloves on and put it into a plastic bag. I guessed for evidence.

"Colt, we need you to come down to the station with us for questioning. The cuffs can go on, or they can stay off. Up to you."

AMBER

My feet were incapable of movement. I saw the flashing lights, I saw the men in blue, but I couldn't physically move. I found myself staring past everyone. They were blurred out, and my head was whirring.

"Ms. Atwood! We need you to come down to the police station for questioning."

My eyes were glazed over, and my mouth dry like cotton. I still managed to reply, "Ah, yes, of course, Officer."

The older officer, ironically, was one that I'd seen in passing. I don't know why I recognized him out of all the others. I looked across to Colt, and our eyes met. He gave me a rueful look. I'd been happy on the way over, wanting to have a conversation to discuss our future together, but now my life seemed to be ruined. What would they say? Colt could go back to jail. There would be a trial. A rival gang member against another one. I would lose my job. So many thoughts ran rampant through my head. All in one breath, I felt like meeting Colt was a cross to bear. I rode in the back of the cop car, and now I was in the position that many of the men I fought for were in. I let out a breath as we rode silently to the police station for questioning.

We were questioned separately at the Merced police station. I hoped that my calling the police would exonerate Colt and me. My hands were shaking as I was taken in for questioning. All I remembered was this man's ankle being shattered. I heard the gunfire.

An officer sat across from me with a tape recorder. "Do you understand your rights, ma'am?"

"Yes, I do," I said solemnly.

The interview process began. The officer sitting across from me was an unassuming, conservative looking man. I waited for him to start.

"Can you tell me your account of what happened, Amber?"

"I was visiting Colt's house, as we are friends, and he invited me to dinner." I felt all sides of my face turning red.

"Friends?" The officer looked at the paperwork in front of him. "Isn't Charlie Winters your client?"

I coughed. "Yes, he is. But his case has been closed for some time, as he has now regained custody over his daughter." A slight lie, but I hoped it would slide through.

He nodded his head as if he understood. It was just me, him, and the tape recorder. "Were you visiting for dinner while you were taking care of Colt's case? Just curious." The conservative brown-haired cop stared at me, watching my movements carefully.

"Yes. I've been invited a few times by his mother and his daughter, Bella."

The officer smiled back at me. "Okay, great. I just wanted to gain an understanding of the situation. Please tell me from the beginning what happened in the stable."

I clasped and unclasped my hands. I took in a deep breath to stop myself from crying.

"Do you need some water? Please, take your time."

"I was heading to the stable because when I knocked on the door to the main house, Colt wasn't there, or I didn't hear that he was there. I headed down to the stables, as I know that he loves his horses. That's usually where you can find him."

"Okay. And then what happened?"

"I saw that a man was pointing a gun at Colt, and his horse was crying out." I saw the image in my mind as I said it. It caused me to break down and cry. The officer handed me a tissue.

"Here you go. It must have been traumatic for you to see that. What happened next?"

"I didn't know what to do or what was happening. I saw Colt shoot the man in self-defense as the other guy raised his gun to him. He fell to the ground, holding his ankle."

Again the officer nodded. "Okay. What did Colt say to you when you saw this?"

"He told me to call his father. That his number was on the fridge in the main house. I'd called you guys first."

"Okay. Where is Bella currently?"

"She was at her grandmother's house. She was due to come back to her father's house tonight."

The officer probed some more. "Do you know the man who shot Colt?"

"No, I do not."

"Okay. And what happened with the horse? Did you see it being shot? Did you witness anything with the horse at all?"

I cried into my hand. "No. No. Just that it was distressed and trying to kick out of its stable."

"Okay. Thank you, Amber. That's enough questioning for now. As you probably know, don't go anywhere or leave the country. We may need you to verify a few things, depending on the situation."

"Okay. Can I see Colt?" I asked, knowing what the answer would be.

"Best that you don't at this point. But once everything is cleared up, you will be able to resume contact."

I liked the way the officer said that. I didn't know if he believed me or not. I had no idea what my future with Colt looked like.

The next day, I went to work in a daze. I had no compass, no direction. I didn't even know if I wanted the promotion that I'd been given. I looked deeply into the eyes of colleagues as I left my stall for lunch. Did they know? Did they hear what happened? The plan I had for Lucy in trying to make her a spokesperson at USP was on hold. I might need a spokesperson, depending on what Colt said. I closed my eyes at my desk, looking at all the positive quotes I had on my wall. I ripped them down in disgust, throwing them in the trash.

"Hey, girl, enjoying your new role?" Lucy came past with her usual spicy comments.

Today, I was full of rage and despair. I turned around and snarled, "Oh, fuck off, Lucy! I'm so tired of your shit. I don't need any more of your backhanded comments."

Lucy stopped in shock. She saw the black rings under my eyes from the sleepless night I'd had and my swollen cheeks. I looked like a trainwreck. I hadn't even brushed my hair. To my surprise, she looked at me in amazement and pity.

"You look like a red-hot mess, Amber. I've never seen you like this. Why don't you take a break with me, and I'll buy you a coffee?"

I searched her face for a hint of betrayal or falseness. I didn't see any there. "Okay. But if you start, I will finish it. I'm not in the mood for it, Lucy. I have bigger fish to fry right now."

"I can see that," she said plainly.

I picked up my purse to walk with her. "You won't need it. I told you I'm buying."

I surrendered and left my bag. I thought about leaving work early, but it would make no difference. I would just sit at home, cry, and wallow in the unfairness of it all.

"Tell me what's going on. Leave nothing out. You gave me a punch in the gut that I needed. Good for you. I've been waiting for you to grow a pair. Finally, you did it. Now, I have a little more respect for you."

We crossed the multi-lane highway at the lights. Cars zoomed past at varying speeds. There was always traffic on this road.

"What the hell are you talking about? I can't believe you just said that."

She laughed off what I said and walked into the coffee shop. There were two small tables outside with umbrellas for people to sit. There were not too many seats because it was just a small coffee shop designed for people to pick up their orders and go. I opted to sit down while she ordered the drinks.

She came back and sat in front of me. She squeezed her hefty figure onto the seat diagonal from me. "Okay, spill, and don't leave anything out. Otherwise, I can't help you." She had on a grim face and was deadly serious.

"How the hell are you going to help me? You don't even know what's going on, Lucy!" I yelled at her.

"All right, I've given you hell long enough, so I probably deserve you yelling at me, but you don't have to much longer, so don't get too worked up."

Numb to her retorts, I started the story. "I went to see Colt, and his horse was going nuts in the stables. Some gangster from Las Balas had shot it. He had a gun and was waving it at Colt. Colt shot him in the ankle to disable him. When he saw me at the barn door, he told me to call the cops and his father for the horse, I guess."

Lucy looked me dead in the eye. "Simple case of self-defense. That's all. They'll work that out. Who was the officer? I might know him."

"Lucy, this is coming out of left field. I thought you hated me."

Lucy gave me a cavalier smile. "The opposite. I've always thought you were too soft, but I can see that you're a fighter. Plus, you secretly like jailbirds. I had that case first, you know...with the cowboy. I sent it your way. I thought you needed some excitement in your drab life." She winked and laughed. "Never thought you would fall in love with the guy."

"Are you serious, Lucy? You were playing matchmaker?"

Lucy put her hand over mine. "Yes. I've been working with you for a long time. You are too nice, Amber, and you take on too much. I just wanted you to live a little. Now I know you have a lot more strength than I thought you had. I underestimated you."

I gave her a wry smile. "You know what's funny is I've been trying to get you into the USP prison because you talked about needing more money for your mother's operation."

Lucy shook her head and drank her coffee, as did I. "Ah, we are a pair, aren't we?"

"Yes, we are. I can't believe you gave me the case."

Lucy spoke and stood up. "I gave you the case because you were the right one for it. Kids and the prison system are your domain."

"I can't believe you. I've wanted to wring your neck this whole time."

Lucy covered her mouth and grinned. "I know. I won't do it anymore. Just know that I'm on your side. I'm sorry to hear about Colt. It's all going to be all right. Is he involved with the Las Balas crew? They are a nasty group. I had to handle the domestic violence case with one of their former crew members."

"I don't know his involvement with the guy. That's the problem. He might be guilty."

"I don't think he would fuck up an opportunity with you for any reason. He just got out."

"You know how it is, though. If one small thing happens while you're on parole, then that's it." I demonstrated with my hands being wiped out.

"Trust me, it's going to work out. You belong with the cowboy. I knew the first time I saw you drop that file."

COLT

"Colt, you know this doesn't look good. You are fresh out." The officer in front of me reiterated what I didn't want to be true. I was at the Merced police station, sitting in a tiny examination room with a tape recorder and a bottle of water in front of me. Both of my hands were in front of me. I was shitting bricks and enraged at the same time.

"I understand, but this fool was on my property, and it was legitimate self-defense. He shot my horse. Can somebody tell me how my horse is doing?" I looked around as if somebody else was in the room. I was losing it a little.

"Nobody is in the room except you and me, Colt. Your horse will be okay, and they will check the bullet. All part of the process. You're not being accused of anything at this point. I just want you to know the position you're in looks suspicious."

I ignored his statement. "Check the bullet in the horse's leg. Betcha bottom dollar it's from the sick fuck's gun."

The livid rage running in my system had me ready to jump up and smash holes in all the walls. My chances of going back to jail were high in my mind. If Hosea talked, I would be dead meat. That's if he was the snitching type. On the other hand, the whole Las Balas operation would be blown open, and I'd seen what they did to snitches.

"All right, Colt, let's start from the top. What happened, and what were you doing in the barn?" The officer sounded tired. He didn't look like much—slight in build, a faint hint of mustache stubble on his face, and delicate fingers.

"I was in the main house."

The officer interjected. "What time was this?"

My mind was like scrambled eggs, my shoulders were starting to knot up like boulders from tension, and my hands shook with anger. "I don't know exactly. Around five or six, I guess. I heard a shot ring out in the barn. I went to see what was going on because my horses started to call out and sound distressed."

"Okay, so you went to check what was happening. Describe the scene," the officer said calmly.

"I went in there and heard my horse screaming, and this guy, Hosea, was in there, and said he came to kill me. That I owed him. I don't owe him shit."

"Wait. How did you know the guy's name?"

"Because he told me."

"Did he tell you why he'd come to kill you?" The officer leaned forward in interest. I might have given him an opening, which I shouldn't have.

"No, he didn't. He was just there." I clenched my jaw, my teeth grinding together from the bullshit questions I was enduring. It was a little white lie. I knew exactly why he was there.

"You were a part of the Outlaw Souls, is that right?" This officer was good. He was leading somewhere.

"I'm not saying anything without my lawyer present. That's what I know. I'm going to call him now, and you can't hold me here." I knew better than to incriminate myself. It was going to be a long haul. I had a lot of calls to make, the way I saw it.

The officer gave me a silent stare. "All right, Colt. Don't go anywhere. We are definitely going to need to speak to you again. You better get your lawyer."

That night, I went home, thinking of all the things I wanted to build. I finally had a chance at life and something to live for, and it was all about to be taken away. Safe to say I had some dark nights after that. My mother tried to talk to me, but I didn't want to speak. I went through the motions in getting Bella ready for school the next day.

The police forensics came along with the vet. My Palomino survived, but he would now have a lame leg, and nobody would be able to ride him. He would be put out to pasture to graze.

I waited with bated breath for the call to be taken in.

One day passed, and then another with no call. I engaged in endless talks with my lawyer about how it might go. I agonized with myself about calling Amber. We hadn't spoken in a few days. I wanted to speak to her, but I didn't want her to be implicated. The love I possessed for her made my stomach ache. I couldn't lose her.

The day of reckoning did finally arrive. I was called back to the Merced police station. My lawyer, this time, was present. He was good, and I trusted him to help me. White walls surrounded me in the meeting room. My lawyer was dressed in a gray suit and was extremely corporate. I was dressed casually and saw no reason to act as if I was guilty. The officer had yet to arrive, and my nerves were so twitchy I wanted to jump out of my skin.

"Colt, let me do all the talking."

"Okay," I said quietly. My life was in this man's hands. I had no other choice in my mind. I wasn't a praying man, but I'd put my hands together on this day and asked for forgiveness for all my sins. It might have been a little too late for that.

The same officer that had sat across from me for the first round of questioning was the one across from me now. The officer came in and sat down. Today he seemed to be a little more upbeat.

"Thanks for being here, gentlemen," he said and gestured to the chair in front of him. A water jug was present on the table along with a tape recorder once again.

"Colt, you're a lucky man. I'm not one for delaying something if I don't need to. All charges against you have been dropped."

My lawyer looked at me with a wide-open grin, and I sat still in amazement. How the hell did they not link me to the Las Balas member?

"Good. My client and I are extremely pleased with the result."

I wanted to ask why, but I knew that would lead to suspicion. I had an inkling of what happened. I nodded, giving the officer a blank face. "Am I free to go now?"

"Yes, you are. We don't need anything else from you."

The officer stood up from his chair. It took me a little while longer to come to my senses. As he opened the door to walk out, he turned to me with a pensive look. "I recommend you keep as far away as you can from any of your old affiliations. You don't want anything coming to bite you in the ass."

"Understood," I replied solemnly. I planned to be nowhere near any of them. Now it was time to go get my girl back if she would still have me.

"Colt, congratulations on getting out of that one. It was a pure case of self-defense. They had no evidence against you. He threatened to shoot you. You had a right to draw your weapon on your own property, and he shot your livestock."

"Thanks, Brian. I appreciate you being there even though

I didn't need you." I'd paid a small fortune to have him attend. Brian charged by the hour. He was one of the best defense lawyers on this side of California. He was the same one that all the Outlaws used. He was more than effective.

Brian tapped me on the shoulder and gave me a crooked laugh. "Hey, well, I still got paid for it. It's been a pleasure, Colt. I want to say I hope to see you again, but I don't. Please take care of yourself. If you need me, you have my number." He winked and walked out of my life with his black suitcase, slipping into his silver Mercedes Benz.

I looked after him, feeling numb. I just wanted to retreat for a while. I sat in my car for a moment and punched the numbers in to make a call. I tried to call Vlad and got no answer. I banged my steering wheel as I weaved through the Merced traffic back home. I knew my father would have questions. He would want to know everything. I felt the heavy weight of the life I lived sinking into my bones—all from selling illegal parts.

My phone buzzed, and I put it on speaker in the car.

"I called you from a burner phone. This is Mikakov. I understand you had some trouble at the farm. This was our fault. We couldn't find the bastard. Sorry. We made sure no more charges could happen. He will be eliminated in jail. We will do the job then like we should have in the first place. We owe you again. But the police. They will never bother you again."

"Mikakov, you should have told me there was another guy," I spat out in anger.

"We saw no reason to tell. We deemed him no threat to you."

"Mikakov, that is bullshit, and you know it."

"Listen. Nothing to be concerned with. I have everything in hand. Enjoy your family time. We will guard the area and send word that we will shoot on sight if anyone else comes.

They will listen. They have no reason to come near you. All debts have been cleared," Mikokov explained in his broken Russian accent.

"I have to go. But yeah, thanks," I said.

He missed the heat in my voice. "You're welcome. Call if you get in trouble. You know where to find us." The phone clicked. This was one of life's moments where I deeply regretted the choice I made. The life of an Outlaw.

My father's car was in my driveway. Time for me to face him. Bella was out front, spinning around in the yard like she didn't have a care in the world. I watched it from a distance. My father was hard at work, putting the fence palings in like nothing had happened.

I shook my head and watched them. I had so much to lose. I should have finished Hosea when I had the chance. I put my car in park and stepped out to face the music. I knew my father would have something to say.

Bella ran to me with her arms out. "Daddy! You're here. Where were you?"

"I had some things to take care of. I'm sorry. Did you have a good time at Grandma's and Grandpa's?" I picked her up on the upswing and held her in my arms. She was getting mighty big.

"I did. I beat Grandpa again. He's not happy with me about it."

"Really?" I touched her little button nose. I was so happy to hold my baby girl. "That's good. Grandpa needs a run for his money."

I let Bella down and walked to my father. He was wheezing a little as he put the next paling in the ground. He had pretty much set up all the posts around the arena. Now it was time for the horizontal timber slats to be put in.

"Hey, Bella, can you give Grandpa and me a minute?"

Bella squinted her eyes at me. "Okay. I'm going to check the horses."

I placed my hand on the pinewood paling and tested its strength. I knew it would irk my father and cause him to look up.

"Don't touch it, boy. I just set it in," he said sternly without looking at my face.

He stopped and leaned on the wooden paling. I braced myself for the lecture of a lifetime. His worn face looked weary and full of worry. I noted the lines furrowed around his eyes.

"You know, I thought about what I would do if you had been shot in that barn. What it would be like for Bella to grow up with both her parents gone. And I cried and cried for my boy." My father shook his head as he took out his handkerchief and wiped the sweat from the back of his neck. "I said that poor girl is going to grow up without her father. She's going to be an orphan. I don't know what you're into, Colt," he said as his eyes looked back at me, searching for an answer, "but you need to get out of it and stay out of it. You've got the ranch. You got yourself a nice girl. You got this place. You got your daughter. What more can a man ask for?"

I looked heavenward and breathed out a sigh. "It was self-defense. The guy was on my property, and I had to do something. The charges were dropped. I served my time, and there's no way I want to go back to prison, Pop. I'm sorry I let you down. All I ever wanted to do was protect my family. To bring in a little more money."

My father broke into tears as if he'd been holding it in. It pained me to see him this way. He clutched on to my shoulder with his thick working-man hands. "Son, never do that to me again. I don't want to lose you. Come here, boy."

A trickle of water fell from my eye as I hugged my father. I didn't let him go for some time.

"I love you, too, Pop. I promise I'm here for the long haul. I won't let anything happen to me. Just an unfortunate incident from the past." I unlocked from his embrace and faced him in the sun.

"Son, if I saw that bastard, and he was here when I was, I would have shot him with my rifle and blown his head clean off. Don't worry about his ankle." My father spoke with a viciousness I'd only witnessed a time or two. I laughed and enjoyed the moment of bonding with him.

"It's over, Pop. I don't know about the nice girl part. Amber might not want to be with me after this."

My father had resumed marking the palings, so he whipped out his measuring tape and lined up his wood. He pulled a black marker out of his top pocket and marked it. "Why wouldn't she? Not like it was your fault that the guy was here."

My father shot me a look, daring me to confirm his statement. A feeling of guilt deep down left me feeling like it was partly my fault. I had to make a call to Amber.

"No, it's not. She's a good girl. She's a social worker."

"No such thing as a good girl. Did I ever tell you about the time your mother got caught with a pound of weed back in the day? This was in the seventies..."

The dread which loomed earlier transformed into storytelling between father and son. I found it hard to concentrate on what my father was saying. Amber was rattling around in my brain, looking for a place to land.

"Pop, I have to handle a few things. I'll be down in the barn, okay?"

My father trotted to the next paling. "Okay, son."

His look told me he understood what I was about to do next. I strode to the barn and found Bella talking to the horses. My special girl was humming to the horses, keeping them company. I scuffled up the dry dirt from the ground, making it past the barn. I wanted privacy.

"Hello," a soft, delicate voice answered the phone.

"Amber, hi. Baby, are you okay? I wanted to call you earlier, but I couldn't. I didn't want you to be implicated."

"I get it." She sounded fed up and weary.

"No charges were filed against me. Not one. Hosea is in lock-up."

Amber coughed uncomfortably. "We seem to cause one another nothing but pain, don't we?"

Fear is not an emotion I had to wrangle with often, but it was rising to the precipice now.

"We have love, Amber, and there's no way I want to live this dream out without you. I need you in my life." I let out my heartfelt plea to her.

"I don't know. This is a lot to deal with. I need some time to think, Colt. Can you give me some time?"

Devastated, I ran one hand through my hair and fought back the tears on the dirt trail path.

"Sure, Amber. Whatever you need."

AMBER

Hopelessly in love is not something I ever thought I would call myself. I did a lot for my community with my social work. I wanted the prison systems to be better. I wanted foster children to feel safe in the homes they were sent to. I wanted perpetrators to be sent to jail if they harmed them. I wanted domestic violence to stop. I fought for justice in a lot of different areas of my life, but never for myself. My relationship with Colt felt like an injustice. Like we would never make it.

I wrestled with myself as I sat on my porch, watching the sun go down. I recognized the guilt I had in my heart from putting him in the situation with Hector. If it wasn't for me asking for his help, that guy wouldn't have been in his barn. He was from that night that they wouldn't tell me about. I put two and two together. I was good at doing that.

I sat silently, listening to the world at dusk, wiping my tears. Could we have a life together? Thing is, I loved Bella. She'd called me after Colt's arrest. I flashed back to the call.

"Hi, Ms. Atwood. I wanted to ask if you would come to dinner soon? I haven't seen you. I miss you."

I gulped down silent tears on the phone. "I'm really busy, but I will try to come and see you really soon. How about that? We can go out for ice cream."

"Yay!"

"Bella?"

"Yes, Ms. Atwood?"

"Don't call me that. Call me Amber. We're friends now."

She repeated it back to me. "We're friends now. Okay. I understand," she said in that sweet little voice of hers. "Amber, can I ask you something?"

I sniffed on the other end of the line. "Yes, honey, what is it?"

"Are you sad about something? You sound like you've been crying."

The set off the motion of another set of tears that I had to fight back. I had to get off the phone. "No, no, no," I lied. "I just have bad allergies. I do have to go, but I will see you soon, darling."

"I hope you come back real soon. Daddy is sad without you here."

"Bye, Bella."

I'd cried for hours after that. What the hell was I supposed to do? The wind picked up, causing me to shiver, shifting my hair over my face. I turned upward to the sky. It looked like a storm was brewing. Funny how California weather could just turn like that. My placemats started to fly off the little ramshackle table I had out front, and the wind began to howl. I wrapped my sweater around me, trying to keep warm.

"Dammit!" I ran after the flimsy cloth placemat into my driveway. I squatted to pick it up. My eyes landed on a pair of tan, detailed cowboy boots. They were attached to thick, toned, muscular legs, most likely from hard work over the years on the farm. I peered up. Colt. He put his boot over the placemat to stop it from flying away.

"Here, let me, little lady." In his hand, he held an assortment of flowers, dainty and all different colors. His pale blue eyes met mine, even with my hair flying everywhere.

"Maybe we should go inside. It's getting kind of windy out here now. A storm is coming in for the night. A bad one, too."

All my doubts melted away as soon as I saw him. "Sure," I called above the wind.

I opened the door to my quaint cottage and assessed him. He looked like something out of a Western. He even had his cowboy hat on. I wanted to leap into his arms and have him take me. The urge was incredibly strong, but I stood tall in front of him. Defiant, almost.

"Colt, what are you doing here? I told you I need time."

Colt's blue eyes blazed true. He saw right through me. He placed his hardworking hands on both sides of my face, taking hard possession over my mouth. I folded under the sensual penetration of his lips. I moaned desperately. We were intrinsically linked in a way I couldn't fathom.

"Colt," I breathed into his mouth as he continued.

"Amber," he let out in an excruciating tone.

The erotic assault continued as he greedily explored the inside of my mouth with his tongue. I matched his passionate energy. I bit his bottom lip, not letting him take the upper hand in the pleasuring. My hands made their way from feeling the hard outline of his tightly muscled chest to resting behind his neck. He wrapped his arms around my waist. We came up for air with the roof rattling from the wind and pelting rain.

"You don't need a break. You need me, and I need you. Simple as that. I told you before, I'm not letting you get away from me like that. I want you to be a part of our lives. The trouble is over. We've made it together through all of this. We can't turn back now. I have a dream of the horse ranch with you on it." He took a breath, and I watched the shadow of his face in the dim darkness. I let him get it off his chest. "Now you don't have to do anything. You don't have to work on the ranch, but Bella and I will run it. I'm going to have the kids come from all over Merced to ride the horses. We have trails on the back of the property that run right into the mountains. You're my family now."

He stood back and ran his hands through his hair. My chest was rising and falling like the wind outside. The door was swinging. I heard it slam, and I jolted. I'd left it open to air out the house after work. Colt didn't flinch.

"I love you so much that I would be okay if we were just friends. I can't lose any more people that mean something to me. I lost Anna. I wasn't there because of my own stupid mistakes. I can't do that again. When I learned she died while I was in prison, it almost broke me. I wanted to hang myself with the sheet. But I didn't. I had Bella to look forward to. Now you. You've made me a better human and taught me something I never knew was possible. True love."

I watched in silence as this man poured his heart out to me. This big tough guy cowboy. "Colt Winters, I don't want to be your friend, and I want to plain slap you for saying that," I replied sassily.

"Slap me, baby. I would be fine with it," he responded in jest.

The corners of my mouth threatened to turn up in a smile. "You're an incredible man. I was just scared, is all. The thought of that guy trying to kill you, and it was my fault. It just drove me insane. I thought it might be best for you and me both." I looked down at the outline of his boots.

"Nope. You have nothing to feel guilty about. You didn't hold a gun to my head. It was my choice, and your brother is a good kid." The rain continued to batter down on the house, and it wasn't the peaceful kind. Colt kneaded my fingers with his, soothing me.

"I want to be with you, too, and I like your plan for the future and us. I want to be a part of it with you and Bella. She called me, you know."

"She did?"

"Yes. She told me how sad you were without me." I smiled slyly at Colt through the darkness.

Colt just laughed. "Now I got a spy in the works. Never ends with you women."

I shook my wild hair in the twilight. "No, it doesn't. Better get used to it. I thought I wanted this promotion at work, but I don't. I've gone back and forth about it for a long time. The job is wearing me down. I want to be free. Every time I come to your property...I don't know, something changes in me."

The windows clanking and moving with the deafening wind caused me to divert from the conversation with Colt. I moved to the kitchen windows to check that they were locked properly. We both realized we were standing in the dark, talking to one another.

"Perhaps we should turn on the light." I giggled. I saw the shadow of a smile on Colt's lips as he flicked on the switch.

The room lit up along with my face. Colt moved around the house deftly, checking all the windows and doors, shutting and securing them. "That's the other reason I came here."

I followed behind him. "For the storm?" I grinned.

"I mean, I was going to use that as an excuse if you tried to send me away. This storm is going to be brutal, and I wanted to check on you. Make sure you were okay," Colt said tenderly.

"Thank you. I'm glad you did. It's kind of scary."

"All part of being in California. If it is not earthquakes or fires, then it's high winds. We'll be okay. We've weathered a storm or two, that's for sure," Colt said.

"You're right. So when are you going to teach me to gallop with the horses?"

Colt smiled as the rain washed away my fears for our future. "As soon as you're ready."

HOPE STONE

When you make a bold declaration to leave something behind in your life, it can be hard for other people to accept. I sat in the parking lot, watching the cars zoom by for minutes, just letting my mind drift. Was this truly what I wanted? Did I really want to throw in the towel of working for the Department of Human Services to be a riding instructor? I would be leaving a huge chunk of my life behind. I looked in the front mirror to face myself.

"Come on, Amber, you can do this."

My knees wobbled as I walked. Donald had just given me the promotion. No one knew I was with a convicted felon in a case that I'd taken over. Nobody knew that I liked the country and wide, open spaces. Hell, I didn't even know until Colt introduced me to it. I would still do my prison advocate work. I had enough of a network from long-established relationships over the years. I wondered if my leaving would ruin my chances.

I breathed in and out as I approached my desk. I thought I might be sick. Inside, I was excited about my new life, but I hated disappointing people. I wanted to grab a coffee from the break room.

"Hi, boss." Tameka smiled at me, cutting me a wink.

"Hey, Tameka." I smiled back at her weakly.

I placed all my things down on the desk. First, a coffee.

Lucy flowed in step with me to the kitchen. We'd cleared the air, and it turned out we had a lot more in common than I thought. "Hey there, boss. I have to run something by you for a case later if that's okay."

"Yes, it's fine. Just might not be calling me boss for much longer." I sighed.

"What do you mean? Didn't Colt get cleared of all charges?" she whispered as we reached the kitchen together.

"Yes. He did. It's not that. I just think—no, I know—that I'm ready for a change. Colt has this riding school he's starting. I think I want to work with the kids out there."

Lucy pursed her lips at me as she put the water on to boil. "Are you serious? Are you sure about putting your eggs into one basket like that?" She eyed me with concern.

"I am. I know I sound crazy."

Lucy pulled a little mint chocolate out of her pocket. "A little something from the conference meeting yesterday."

I took it from her gladly. I needed a little sweetness before I delivered the bitter news to my boss.

"No, I don't think you're crazy, by the way. You're following your heart. Maybe just ease into it. You don't know how long it's going to take before he gets it going. Don't you need to learn to ride first?"

"I mean, yes and no. I used to ride when I was a little girl. I used to get lessons."

"Oh, wow. You really are meant to be with a cowboy." Lucy elbowed me as I poured our coffees.

I shrugged. "I'll take it."

"Well, you can sign me up for the first lesson once it gets going. I want to see these trails. Plus, you know I love sticking my nose in other people's business."

"Yeah you do," I giggled. "What do you think I should tell Donald?"

"That you want to work part-time. You are more valuable than anyone in this department. Even if you don't want the promotion, he would be a fool to let you go."

"I know, but I already accepted the job. You still want that prison advocacy role if I can create it?"

"No. I don't want you to get me a job. I'm happy right where I am. Like I said, I was just giving you hell because I could."

I shook my head. "Lucy, you are something else, you know that?"

"Yes, I'm aware, honey." She sauntered away with her coffee in hand.

I took my mug of coffee with me and rapped my knuckles on Donald's door. It was open.

"Come in. My door is always open, you know that. Please take a seat."

I closed the door behind me. "I feel like this is a closed-door conversation."

Donald's face was peering into his computer screen. He was in his normal position, buried under a mountain of paperwork.

"Okay, hit me with it. Got a tough case we need to work on? Training? What is it?"

I fumbled around for the right words.

"I'm moving in a new direction."

"I quit."

"It's time for me to make a change."

"I'm getting older and..."

I let a moment pass, and that raised concern as Donald looked up at me. "Go ahead, I'm listening."

"Donald. I think you should give the promotion to someone else. I'm quitting. I want to move in a new direction."

Donald's mouth dropped open, and his eyes blinked rapidly. I watched his Adam's apple bob up and down. "You're leaving us? When and how did this happen? I only just gave you the promotion!" A flabbergasted look crossed his face as he waved his hands in the air.

"Listen. I'm not leaving right away. I'm willing to continue for the next six months. I'll give you a long lead time. As you know, Donald, this job can take its toll. I want to pursue other things in my thirties, and I feel it's time."

Donald's face started to return to normal. "You've met someone, haven't you? Women always come into my office either for babies or because they've met someone."

I sighed. "Yes, I have met someone. That might be part of it, but I still feel like it's time for me to go. To move on now."

"Okay. I will have to find a replacement for you, and that will take some time. Not that you can be replaced." Donald gave a wry smile. "You are loved in the department, Amber. But I do understand. I have a family of my own, and I sometimes wonder whether I should continue."

"You do?"

"Yes. It's a hard slog, and this job can really take its toll on you. But you handle everything in your stride. What will you be doing if you don't mind me asking?"

"I will be on a ranch, helping out and running horse trail rides for kids. Well, I hope to."

Donald nodded in appreciation. "That sounds about right. I knew it would have to involve children or something like that."

"Thanks for understanding."

"Hey, you're welcome. Not much I can do about it. You'll have a nice little unused vacation pay built up, too, since you never take off."

"Yes. That will help."

I smiled and made my way out of the office. I floated out. A new chapter of life was forming for me, and I wanted to run through the office in happiness.

COLT

"Pop, do you think people are going to want to come out here and try this?" I readjusted the brim of my cowboy hat. The Merced sun was showing no mercy to us today.

My father, with his broad hardworking shoulders, bent backward, stretching out his spine. He'd just hand-drilled all the fences together. All the slats were on, and it looked damn good.

"Son, take a look around you. There's nothing better than what you have here. This is the land I passed on to you so you could do something like this." He spread his arms wide in reference to the property. "All of those years ago, I knew what it could be. You've taken it one step further here."

He pointed to the arena. "You're sitting on four hundred and forty acres. I inherited this land from my father, and he from his. This place is sacred, ancestral land. Anyone who comes here feels right at home. Wouldn't you agree?"

"I guess when you put it that way, you're right. It's a special place." I pulled my hat up and wiped the sweat from under my brim, where my hair was slicked to my forehead.

I looked into the distance. California rolling hills encapsulated the property. Behind those California hills sat the foreboding mountain peaks. My neighbors weren't particularly close by, and that was fine by me. The paddock on the left had been transformed into a circular arena for participants to practice their riding skills, including leading the horses around it. It was for learning to trot and canter. I would leave the galloping for the trails.

"Damn straight. You're going to need some help with the crops this year if this gets running right. You're going to need a new stable, too, for the extra horses."

I tipped my hat to my father, his silver hair shining bright in the sun. He'd always been a straightforward man. Planning for the future.

"You're right. I have the new horses coming in. I have to get Bella to help me feel them out. We got two more. I think Moonlight is more settled now that I'm home. I can put an experienced rider who likes a challenge on her."

My father nodded at my suggestions. I loved working alongside the old man. He was one of my greatest inspirations.

"You know what irks me, son?" He patted the soil for the arena. As he grabbed it, it turned to dust. "You never named those goddamn Palominos. They need names. How are your riders going to know?"

"Good point. I just know them by their features. One of them has a chunk out of its ear. It got in a fight with the other one."

"Uh-huh. And the other two?"

"Well, one has a longer tail than the rest. The third one loves to eat carrots more than the rest. If I gave it an endless supply of carrots, it would live on them."

My father sniffed and smoothed out the dusty ground under his feet. As soon as I mowed back the paddock, the heat got to it, keeping the soil dry. It's what I wanted—a harder surface. "See, there you go. Get young Bella, the horse whisperer, to name them."

"I will. That's a great idea. You really want to run the farm side? I thought you were done with it."

"So did I, but I feel the excitement coming back. I wanted to play around with a few other hobbies of mine, but the land keeps calling me. Plus, I want to be here when you start with the horses. I want to see how young Bella goes. Not you. I taught you already. We're making history. Three generations of horsemen and horsewomen. Have to be politically correct these days." He puffed his chest out proudly.

I grinned. "I never thought of it like that. I can't wait."

"I know we aren't talking young kids here. You don't have ponies. Unless you want to get some."

"No, I guess I've meant the riding school to work with a little older age bracket."

"Good, good. Work with the horses you got. What's the new horse you got coming?"

"A couple of beauties. One smaller chestnut and one bigger chestnut."

My father's eyes lit up. "Two chestnuts. They will be something to behold. I'll give you some tips to keep their coats nice and shiny. They can get a little dull in the sunshine."

"I'm glad we're working together, Dad."

He pressed his lips together. "It's how it should be done. Father and son working together. Come on. I'm hungry, and I need you to whip me up one of those toasted sandwiches you've become good at making."

"All right, let's go, old man."

I admired my property as we walked. I could hear the water rushing on the east side. You had to walk down the side to get near it. If there was enough water from the mountain, it ran down. Spring flowers were blooming bright in the front yard. The bees were out in full force, buzzing around, collecting their nectar.

We ate lunch and filled our stomachs, and we talked farm shop, discussing what we might need for the stables in the way of equipment. We also discussed that we might need a stable hand to help with the horses. By the time he left, it was time for daddy duties and to pick Bella up from school.

My phone buzzed as I wrote down everything we talked about. I retrieved my phone from my pocket, a knot forming when I saw it was Diego.

"Hey, Diego. How are you, brother?"

"Hey, I'm good. Really good. I heard a rumor, and I wanted to hear if it was true."

"Go ahead. Hit me with it."

Diego paused. "Are you starting a riding school?"

"Yes. I am." I was puzzled by the call.

"When are you opening? Back in Argentina, I rode when I was a little boy. I wouldn't mind doing it again."

"You want to be in? You can ride anytime, though, Diego. It would be free. No charge."

"No. I'm bringing a crew with me. You know, to help advertise. You've taken enough losses. Hector has turned out to be a good worker. He brought in some new business, too. Let me help out. We Spanish like a horse or two."

I laughed. I was touched by the call. "I'm glad that's what the call was about. I didn't want any bullshit," I warned.

"Relax, brother. Ryder is pissed with Vlad for letting the Russians let that little bitch get away. He's on punishment." Diego laughed.

"I don't care if he is or not. Just keep Las Balas crew away from my property. That's what he promised. I'll die for mine. Either that or I'm going back to prison."

"Neither. Not going to happen. You have a lot going for you. We can't let that happen."

"Sorry to cut it short, Diego. Give me a couple of weeks, and I'll have a date you can bring them through."

"Okay, brother. Take care."

"You, too."

I had the support of the brotherhood—good to know. I grabbed my car keys to pick up Bella. As I drove to pick up my baby girl, I hoped I'd seen the last of all the shooting and violence. I'd seen and been around enough to last me a lifetime. I waited patiently as I heard the schoolyard bell ring. Ten minutes later, I saw Bella bounce out of the front doors with a bookbag twice the size of her. I would need to do something about that. She opened the car door.

"Daddy! Guess what?"

I grinned as she hugged me. "What, baby?"

"In two weeks, we have bring a parent day! Will you come?"

"What's a parent day about?" I asked as I pulled off into the Merced streets.

"You come in and talk about what you do. You can talk about our horses and the farm. I told my friends to come and ride with us," she said confidently. I saw her beautiful eyes light up as she started kicking her legs around like she does when she's excited.

I squeezed her little leg, and she giggled. "Daddy, that tickles!"

"I think that's a great idea. I would love to. Just remind me when it is. We got two new horses coming next week, too. I need you to name them. I think you should name the Palominos, as well."

She hummed, her little voice music to my ears. "I did already."

Surprised, I raised my eyebrows as we turned into our driveaway. "You named the horses already?"

"Yes." She smiled and kept humming. My kid was a trip.

"What did you name them?"

"Let's go inside, and I'll tell you," she giggled.

"Okay, you win."

I parked the car, and we stepped inside.

"Can I have a ham and cheese sandwich for a snack?"

"Yes, honey, you can." I opened the fridge, and Bella ducked under my arm to get the ingredients out. "You still haven't told me the names of the horses."

"Okay." Bella grabbed a piece of cheese and bit into it, sneakily looking at me to see if I would be mad. I just smiled at her.

"One of the horses has a long tail, so I named him Long Straw. The other one has the hole in its ear, so I named it Nip. The third one is Caramel."

Bella saw what I saw for the most part. Her names made me double over in laughter. "You are so clever. You named him Long Straw."

"Daddy, you're going red in the face. Yup. Long Straw."

I wiped the laughing tears from my eyes. "I can't help it. I never knew about these names. How come?" I buttered the toast on both sides, added the ham and cheese, then placed the sandwiches in the waffle maker. These prison sandwiches that I learned to make ended up being a hit with Bella.

"Because you didn't ask me," Bella replied simply. "I'm putting my book bag away." She stamped off and came back minutes later.

"You are one awesome little human."

"Thanks, Dad. You're not bad yourself."

"Thanks, kid. Things are going to start happening around here pretty quickly. Lots of people coming and going. Are you ready for that?" I asked her as I plated her ham and cheese sandwich.

"Yes. I think it will be fun. I want to ride all the way on the trail. I can ride Moonlight."

A string of cheese hung from her lips, and I wiped it with my free hand. "Hmm. I don't know about that. Moonlight is sensitive, so you have to catch her on the right day to ride. I don't want you getting bucked off her."

"I won't. She listens to me, and she talks back."

"You can talk to horses?"

She nodded her head as more cheese dripped from her chin. This time she caught it.

"Your grandpa used to do the same thing."

"Can you speak to them, Daddy?"

"Not speak, but I can feel if they are going to do something. Like buck me off." I smirked.

"You'll be okay. Moonlight just doesn't like it if you don't ride her. She likes the sunshine. Says you don't ride her enough."

"You are the cutest." My daughter was a horse whisperer. "Your mother would be proud."

"I miss Mommy. She made me laugh. I wish she would come back. But I like Amber, too."

I took her one of her little hands in mine. "You can like them both. Nobody will ever replace your mother, but Amber is your friend now, and you can talk to her, too."

"I know. I really like her. She's nice to me."

"I like her, too. What would you think if I married her?"

"Yay! Can I be the flower girl?"

"You sure can."

Even gunslinging cowboys need love.

EPILOGUE: AMBER

Six Months Later

The Merced sky was an incredibly vivid blue, and the sweet, melodic sounds of birdlife filled my ears. I was standing in the middle of a fully enclosed horse arena built by Colt and his father. At the entry was a red and white flag with the outline of Moonlight on it. At the front of the property, I'd helped paint the sign for Colt Trail Rides. I couldn't be prouder. Colt put me through the wringer, riding every morning until I got used to all the horses. When I touched the inside of my thighs, I felt like they weren't there.

Then, a week before we were due to open, he said in his Colt way, "I think you're ready."

Two weeks before the opening, we were booked out for a whole month. Both Colt and I couldn't believe it. We were both sitting on the couch in the living room, counting all the bookings.

"Can you believe this is happening? We are fully booked!"

"No. I can't. This is crazy. Wow. You did it, Colt!"

"Baby, I couldn't have done it without you." I smiled wide and big as I thought of the memory. Colt and I were going

EPILOGUE: AMBER

from strength to strength, growing and getting to know one another more deeply.

Fast forward to the day of our official opening. I was nervous. Colt was nervous. Clive was fumbling around with last minute things in the barn. Cheryl was baking muffins for morning tea. We had a full schedule. I was taking the role of administration, bookings, and specific groups.

"The arena looks great, baby. I can't believe you built this in such a short amount of time. I'm really proud of you."

Colt wrapped his thick muscular arms around me, kissing me like it was his last breath.

"What was that for?"

His blue eyes were the same color as the sky. "For sticking by me and believing in me."

I touched the side of his face with my finger. "I know you're a good man, Colt. I was always going to stand by you. What happened was self-defense."

"Yes, it was. That guy came back from the dead. I thought the Russians took him out. But that's not the only reason. Or the only situation. The whole way through, you had my back."

"That's what you do for the ones you love." I meant it.

My life was just beginning. I quit after seven years of social work, with a twist. I started a collaboration project with the Department of Human Services for young men and women to ride for self-esteem. Psychological studies showed that communicating with horses was good for emotional healing and trauma. I wanted to give some of the foster kids some hope. So I led the groups on trail rides. Nothing fancy, just trotting along the trail. If nature could be soothing for me, then it could be soothing for kids and young adults.

I was nervous to ask Colt about it. I didn't know if he thought it would work. I danced around him in the kitchen one night.

EPILOGUE: AMBER

"Amber, what is going on with you? You're all jittery and acting funny. Tell me." Colt pulled me close to him, and I melted as I always did in his presence.

"I thought I could run a program with the foster kids to ride. I want to still be involved. Do you think we could add that to the schedule?"

Colt didn't bat an eye. "Of course we can. That's a brilliant idea. Were you scared to tell me that?"

"Not scared. I just didn't know what you would think."

He kissed me hard on the lips, leaving me breathless. I was more in love with him than ever.

"Well, I'm glad you asked, anyway."

Now Colt and I walked around the ready-made arena, checking for pockets that the horses might fall in. "I feel somewhat responsible. If I didn't get you mixed up with helping my brother, you wouldn't have been in that situation."

"You're kidding, right? If I hadn't shipped illegal car parts on behalf of the Outlaws, I would never have been in jail. If I was never in jail, I never would have met the love of my life. Every single thing in life happens for some reason or another. Sometimes, we don't understand why until later, but still."

"Colt Winters, my reckless cowboy, when did you become so wise?"

"Right about now." Colt stomped his feet over certain sections of the grass, making sure it was just right. It looked like a mini horse ranch. Transformed from a free-flowing paddock to this. "I'm determined to make this work, and with you by my side, I can do anything."

Some days Colt's intensity blew me away. He was a force all his own. I watched as he prepared the saddles, and the older version of Colt stepped forward to the arena.

"You got the mic?" Clive asked.

"Yes, I do, Pops. Fully charged."

Clive appeared to age backward. Ever since he'd been

EPILOGUE: AMBER

working on the farm with Colt, he seemed so happy and content. He was a man who belonged to the land for sure. Crop season was fast approaching, and Cheryl had a handle on that. Workers came and went from the property daily, and the back fields transformed into rows of uniform food crops. Colt's home was a hive of activity.

Colt couldn't stand still. "What if they don't show up? What do I do?"

I grabbed his hand. I knew how to keep him calm when he got agitated. "It's going to be all right. Think about it. They've already paid their money. They are going to show up. Breathe, baby."

Colt squeezed my hand back. "You're right, and I know you're right."

I walked the first group in. Four people in total, a family. Clive greeted them with a handshake. Each one of us agreed that we would help each person mount onto a horse and take them around the arena.

I smiled. "Welcome to Colt Trails. We're happy to have you here."

Clive and Bella walked each horse out, one by one.

"Hello, my name is Rosa. I've never been on a horse before. My hubby made me come today." Rosa, a lady with long brown hair and a sweet face, gasped as the majestic creatures emerged. Her husband grinned.

"Look, baby, we're going to ride them." He pointed to Chester, who was aptly named after his coat. He was one of the new horses, and one with a whole load of personality. Colt tipped his cowboy hat at me, and Bella gave me the thumbs-up as I showed Rosa how to mount the horse and led her around the arena.

"Hey, Marcos, let's get you on the horse, buddy." Colt took around his participant.

Bella and Clive took the teenagers. The whole time, my

EPILOGUE: AMBER

heart beat in my chest as I wondered if I would be able to guide these unsuspecting people around the arena. I did, and it was the best feeling ever. My stress levels were down. I looked younger, and Colt made me feel free.

After the arena, all riders were confident enough so that we could take them out on a one-hour trail ride to experience the beauty of the Californian woodlands. The pride I felt was immeasurable. I was with a man who stretched me to new potential. One who I was proud to be standing beside. After the first class left, we had two hours between.

Colt ran over and lifted me into the air. "We did it!"

We had a celebratory iced tea in the California sun. I even wore a cowboy hat that I'd picked out. The Winters family and I were a winning team. Clive grinned from ear to ear. Bella jumped up and down, dancing around the arena. The horses swished their tails, wondering what all the fuss was about. Our first four people were so happy with that ride that they vowed to come back with more people.

Once we had the first class done, the rest of the day rolled like clockwork, and we were a hit. The local papers caught wind months later, which brought more publicity and more bookings. My department program was a hit with the younger foster groups, and I included a session after it to help them. I would never forget the day Donald, my old boss, brought the whole team for a ride.

Lucy, hot, disgruntled, and reluctant strolled in first. "What the hell did he bring me here for?" She changed her tune when she saw Colt. She looked around me and scanned Colt up and down like a piece of candy. "Oh, sweet Lord, ain't he something to look at? Wow. Now I see why you're working here. Plenty of incentive."

"Colt, could you help Lucy mount her horse?" I winked at him, and he winked back. Lucy's eyes became wide with fear as she struggled for her words. Lucy never was short on

EPILOGUE: AMBER

words, ever. The whole ride was hilarious. It turned out she'd become the new head of the department and was doing a great job.

Hector was working on bikes non-stop with Diego and was happy. He came to visit every now and then. He even had a nice girlfriend and an apartment. Life just kept getting better. USP Atwater listened to my advice and received the grant I told them to go for. They were fixing up the cell floors one by one.

Five months later, we had a rare off day. Colt and I were preparing for a trail ride to one of the watering holes we discovered on the last ride. This was his first time bringing Moonlight out for a ride.

"You sure you want to take Moonlight? Are you comfortable?" I asked.

We were standing in the barn, and Colt's white cowboy hat was sloped forward in a sexy way, covering his face. He'd become even more muscular if it was possible, working around the farm and taking care of the horses. We had eight now and had expanded the stable with Clive's help. We were working side by side, feeding the horses at the time. I was feeling a little off. Nothing would stop me riding with my man, though. As I glimpsed his straining bicep muscles, I was becoming more and more turned on. He must have felt my eyes burning into him because he turned and gave me a little grin.

"See something you like?" He laughed as he brushed Moonlight.

"I see plenty I like." I batted my eyelashes at him as he leaned in for a hot kiss. Then it was his turn to stare.

"What is it?" I said playfully.

"I want to show you something," he said quietly. "Hang on."

He pulled Moonlight out of the stable and held the reins.

EPILOGUE: AMBER

Moonlight adversely reacted at first. Then Colt spoke to her, and she settled. She was one mighty looking horse. Her saddle was already on, and Colt reached inside the leather saddlebag. I was happy it was just another day of happiness and contentment with Colt, but he seemed to have something else on his mind.

He pulled out a small blue velvet box. I watched it as if I was in a movie. Colt moved to a bended knee. He licked his lips and took off his white cowboy hat, laying it beside him. He peered up with the sincerity of a small child and took my right hand.

"Amber Atwood. You are an angel to me. I know we didn't meet in the best place, but for me, it was love at first sight. I wanted to be with you as soon as I saw you. I had to have you." Colt's impassioned speech made my eyes start to well up with tears. "We have been through a thing or two, and I love you more now than ever. I want to continue loving you for the rest of my life. I want to spend forever with you. I know Bella loves you, too. Amber, will you marry me?"

I let the tears fall in the barn. They were tears of joy. "Yes. I will. I would like nothing more than to spend my life with you. I hope that Bella is okay with another sibling because we have a baby on the way."

"Oh, honey! I love you so much. This is amazing." Colt jumped up and hugged me tightly, lifting me in the air. Even the horses chimed in and neighed.

"Wait, baby, what about the ring?"

Colt fumbled with the small ring box in his hand. "Yes. Oh, I messed up. You just threw me. I didn't expect that."

His breathing had increased, and I put my hand on him to calm him. I gave him a reassuring smile and stroked his face. "You and me both."

"Here we go. Let me slip this on before I pass out. Wow. I'm going to be a father all over again." With quivering hands,

EPILOGUE: AMBER

Colt slid a sparkler on my hand that made me hold my breath. It was a traditional white diamond with a silver band. It was classic and beautiful, and just right for me.

One thing was for sure. My cowboy was full of surprises, and we were destined for one hell of a ride!

Read on for a sneak peek of **OUTLAW SOULS BOOK 7** featuring the MC's enforcer, Michael "Moves" Jagger, who is about to embark on a journey that will determine whether the MC prospers or crumbles. Moves will stop at nothing until he finds the truth and makes sure that the Outlaw Souls get to walk free, but nothing could've prepared him from running into a beautiful woman that would change his life.

Buy now!
FREE with Kindle Unlimited.

Thank you so much for reading this book. If you liked **TRAINER, please leave a review for it now.**

Join My Newsletter
Click here to sign up for my newsletter for deals, sneak peeks, and more.

SNEAK PEEK! MOVES (OUTLAW SOULS BOOK 7) CHAPTER ONE

Moves

I heard the incessant whirring of my phone, sinking beneath the covers of my bed while I subconsciously tried to go back to sleep. Though, something clicked inside my mind, jolting me up while I fished around to retrieve it. I hurriedly answered it, waiting for it to connect while I listened to the voice operator ask me if I'd like to accept the charges.

"Hello?" I asked, groggily.

"Hey, it's me. I've gotten myself into a little bit of trouble here. Look, I've only got one phone call, and they're riding me pretty hard here. It's not often one of us gets pinched like this. I'm sorry to ask Moves, but I need your help," said a voice on the other end of the line, the connection of the call barely hanging on by a thread.

"I'll get you out. We're all family remember?" I reminded him, knowing quite well that there would be no way I'd leave him behind.

"I'm sorry, brother. I'm just a little over my head here. I don't know what to do. I'm not going to last in prison man," he said, and I could hear the fear in his voice, but I wasn't going to let it come to that.

"Whatever is going on, I'm going to get to the bottom of it. Okay? I need you to hang tight. They're not going to let you out of there until morning at least, so you stay strong okay. I'll make sure you have a place to go once I get you out of that hell hole," I said, and my words seemed to calm him down a bit.

"Thank you, Moves," he said, hanging up the phone, and I could feel the reluctance through the line. I knew what it was like for him to be scared, especially because the police were always trying to ride our asses, and I could tell that he was far from innocent. I taught many of the men riding in the Outlaw Souls that we needed to cover our tracks, because the more we had the LPPD housing us, the harder it would be to go about living our normal lives. I had faith that everything was going to be fine, but I needed to keep my head on straight, take care of a little business first before I managed to head back to bed.

I'm no use to Chalupa right now because they won't even let me post his bail this early. I hate leaving him in there, but there's really nothing else I could do. I decided to head over to the small fridge in my dingy apartment, grab a beer out of the fridge, and head out back to give my bike a tune-up. *I wonder what they did with yours, Chalupa. There's no way we're going to risk breaking it out if its been impounded.* I thought, looking down at the hunk of metal before me, reminding myself that it was these bikes that bound us together for lives. We really were a family, and no amount of pain or grief was going to change that.

I wasn't the same person after Padre died, and I struggled to keep my head above water sometimes, especially now that the police were hot on our trail. I sat under the moonlight, feeling the cool air of approaching dawn brush against my skin while I got to work. I wiped the sweat off my forehead,

COLT

making sure everything was in pristine condition before heading back inside to sleep off the rest of my frustration. I tossed and turned on the creaky mattress, remembering how awful it felt the day Padre died. I hated that I couldn't shake those feelings when they crept up inside of me, because he was the President, a father to us all, leading the Outlaw Souls to triumph.

I wasn't high on the list, but I didn't really care to be, because I enjoyed my position enforcing the rules, making sure everyone stayed in line, but we all just felt better when Padre was around. We had that increased sense of brotherhood amongst us all, and that was starting to dwindle in his absence. I was doing what I could to keep everyone in check, but we all had heavy hearts to lose one of our own. We marked our territory in La Playa, and it was the only place that ever felt like home to me. No matter how much trouble we got ourselves into, how many drug deals went wrong, or how much money we lost, we always had each other's backs.

Padre would want me to make sure that I get Chalupa out of there before something bad happens. If they have any solid evidence against him, this is going to be one hell of a ride. I thought, wondering what he could've done that led the police to his tail, but I could've already guessed. I worried that with Chalupa locked up, there are going to be some members who are going to want to halt business until it's taken care of, but I'm not sure that many of them know what has happened yet. I thought that it was probably best I keep things under wraps until I know for sure where all of this is headed. I couldn't fall back asleep, my eyes catching sight of the steady stream of sunlight filtering in through the patched window in my bedroom, while I tossed the covers aside, running my hand through my sweat-doused hair, ready to get Chalupa out of jail.

HOPE STONE

Next time, I hope you do a better job keeping things on the low, Chalupa, because I'm not sure how many more lies the LPPD is going to believe before they start hunting us down one by one.

SNEAK PEEK! MOVES (OUTLAW SOULS BOOK 7) CHAPTER TWO

Lacey

The day started out like normal, sitting at my desk going through an obscene amount of paperwork, holding the pen between my teeth while I scrambled to get everything done in a timely fashion.

I've been a prosecuting attorney for the City of La Playa for such a long time that I sometimes forget how heavily involved I get in every case I take, and I'm certainly one that likes a full catalogue of solved cases rather than letting some slip through the cracks.

Everyone in my life had always told me that I needed to let loose every once in a while, and that I shouldn't let work consume my entire life, but the truth was if I wanted to continue being good at my job, I had no choice. It wasn't often that the cases I took on were free of thrills, and there was usually something new to be discovered at every corner. We had a pretty good dynamic going in the office, and the criminals we prosecuted never usually got away with their crimes.

I sat at my desk, hearing a knock on my door from the

ADA himself, slipping in with a cup of hot coffee in his hand, the steam rising up into his face.

"Hello, Lacey," he said.

"Don't you have anything better to do than slip in here to see what I'm up to, Richard?" I asked, and he smiled back at me, taking a seat comfortably in the chair in front of my desk, staring back at me while I continued to work.

"You've been here late every night, Lacey. You know, some of us manage to get all our work done and still head out there and try to put ourselves back on the market. You're a catch, and it doesn't make sense why you're not out there dating right now," he said, teasing me about my lack of relationship status even though he knew nothing was going to change.

"You and I both know that I'm already romantically involved with my job, and with all the time I spend backlogging cases, I really don't have time to be dating anyone. Or would you rather I let my performance at work suffer for someone to take me out to dinner?" I asked, glaring at him.

"Now, I don't think that it has to be one or the other. You are perfectly capable of handling them both, and Know it's been a while since you've been out on a date, but you need it. Trust me, I see how frustrated you are everyday, how exhausted you are when you return to the office the next morning after a long night, and you need a break."

"I don't have time for a break, Richard," I replied, running through a few files in the filing cabinet near my desk.

"Think about it, Lacey. What's the point of doing all this great work if you don't have someone to share your successes with? You're a great prosecutor, and you deserve to have a little fun too is all. I want to set you up with someone I think you might like, and it may help take some of the edge off around here," he said, and I knew he meant well, but a blind date really wasn't in the cards for me with all the work I still had yet to get done.

"I don't think so. Not something I'm interested in, Richard but I genuinely appreciate the effort," I said.

"Suit yourself, Lacey, but the offer stands," he replied, getting up to leave my office. I knew quite well that he wasn't going to stop teasing me until I put myself out there again, but it was something I was willing to deal with because my heart was in my work. I couldn't see myself coming home to someone, telling them about how work was, not being able to divulge any of the real details, only to pretend that this job is not absolutely exhausting. I love what I do, but I wasn't ready to share that part of me with anyone, and frankly, I didn't think that love would ever be something I indulged in. I just didn't have the time for it.

I sighed, grabbing my lunch, bringing it back to eat it at my desk while I continued going through cases. I thought a lot about what Richard said, but I didn't have it in me to go out with this friend of his, especially because Richard knew absolutely nothing about what kind of men I was interested in. I decided it would be best to call up someone who genuinely understood me, and get everything off my chest. I called my best friend, Mona, hoping that she would be able to side with me on this one, because anyone that Richard would've picked for me to go on a date with would probably be just as self-obsessed as he was.

"Hey, Lacey! You're still at the office, what could you possibly be calling me about?" she asked, pretending not to know that this was a regular thing we liked to do.

"It's okay, there's no one around. Richard is trying to set me up with someone, telling me that I needed to take a break every once in a while, and put myself back out on the market. Is he crazy? There's no way any work would get done if I spent all my time running after men who had no idea what they wanted and would end up disappointing me anyway," I said, rambling over the phone while she listened attentively before chiming in.

"Richard is right, Lacey. You really are married to your job. It wouldn't hurt to let yourself go every once in a while, and you might even find that you feel a bit more refreshed when you return to work, instead of being so uptight all the time," she said.

"Ouch," I said, jokingly.

"I tell you these things because I love you, and I don't want to see you crash and burn," she replied.

"I feel like I'm crashing and burning all the time, Mona. You know that this job is hard, I'm constantly burned out, and let's not forget that I originally wanted to be a defence attorney, but instead I ended up working for the government," I said, wallowing in my sorrow, while she continued to try lifting me up.

"I know, Lacey. You have to remember that you're incredible at your job, and I don't think there's anyone that can do what you can. That fire you have inside of you isn't going anywhere, even if you took a break every once in a while," she said, and it was the first time that I was starting to warm up to the idea.

"I'll think about it," I replied, realizing that she might have a point.

Is there really room for balance in a life like this, or am I just kidding myself?

I can't wait for you to find out what happens with Moves and Lacey...

**Purchase MOVES (OUTLAW SOULS BOOK 7)
FREE with Kindle Unlimited.**

ALSO BY HOPE STONE

All of my books are currently available to read FREE in Kindle Unlimited. Click the series link or any of the titles to check them out!

Guardians Of Mayhem MC Series

Book 1 - Finn

Book 2 - Havoc

Book 3 - Axle

Book 4 - Rush

Book 5 - Red

Book 6 - Shadow

Book 7 - Shaggy

LEAVE A REVIEW

Like this book?
Tap here to leave a review now!

Join Hope's newsletter to stay updated with new releases, get access to exclusive bonus content and much more!

Join Hope's newsletter here.

Tap here to see all of Hope's books.

Join all the fun in Hope Stone's Readers Group on Facebook.

ABOUT THE AUTHOR

Hope Stone is an Amazon #1 bestselling author who loves writing steamy action packed, emotion-filled stories with twists and turns that keep readers guessing. Hope's books revolve around possessive alpha men who love protecting their sexy and sassy heroines.

Learn more about all my books here.

Sign up to receive my newsletter. You'll get free books (starting with my two-book MC romance starter library), exclusive bonus content and news of my releases and sales.

If you liked this book, I'd be so grateful if you took a few minutes to leave a review now! Authors (including myself) really appreciate this, and it helps draw more readers to books they might like. Thanks!

COLT: AN MC ROMANCE
Book Six in the Outlaw Souls MC series
By Hope Stone

© Copyright 2020 - All rights reserved.

It is not legal to reproduce, duplicate, or transmit any part of this document in either electronic means or in printed format. Recording of this publication is strictly prohibited and any storage of this document is not allowed unless with written permission from the publisher except for the use of brief quotations in a book review.

This book is a work of fiction. Any resemblance to persons, living or dead, or places, events or locations is purely coincidental.

Printed in Great Britain
by Amazon